SLENDERMAN

BOOK DESCRIPTION

When children disappear and citizens are murdered in a Lake Michigan resort town, will a citizen reporter and her quirky sidekick cousin be able to stop what witnesses describe as a faceless, tall skinny man in a black suit before grief and death touch everyone in town?

Citizen reporter Pacie Rose is in her strawberry with her family when Irma, her offbeat sidekick cousin, calls and reports that there's been a child abduction in town. They take on the self-appointed case of finding the culprit while murders and another missing child pile up. Armed with tools from the priest and local college professor, they are ready to confront the thing that witnesses describe as a tall man who wears a black suit and who appears to have no face.

The resort town of Black Water is inundated with so many weird events that Pacie Rose took up being the town's citizen reporter. With her quirky cousin as the sidekick, they work to assist authorities in solving cases. Not bound by institutional rules, they can investigate using "not so legal" ways to get information.

The Potawatomi have told of strange occurrences in the area long before the construction of the nuclear power plant in the 1960s. However, ever since Bulwark became operational, aberrations have increased substantially. Missing people, cryptids, UFOs, the paranormal, and alternate dimensions are just a few of the mysterious encounters.

Follow Pacie as she works to rid Black Water of the terrifying phenomena.

BONUS: My Name Is Mr. Dibble and Jezebel companion short stories are included.

SLENDERMAN

PACIE ROSE MYSTERIES, #1

Connie Myres

ConnieMyres.com
FEATHER AND FERMION PUBLISHING

FEATHER AND FERMION PUBLISHING

CONNIE MYRES/FEATHER AND FERMION PUBLISHING

MICHIGAN, USA

CONNIEMYRES.COM

PUBLISHER'S NOTE: THIS IS A WORK OF FICTION. NAMES,
CHARACTERS, PLACES, AND INCIDENTS ARE A PRODUCT OF
THE AUTHOR'S IMAGINATION. LOCALES AND PUBLIC NAMES
ARE SOMETIMES USED FOR ATMOSPHERIC PURPOSES. ANY
RESEMBLANCE TO ACTUAL PEOPLE, LIVING OR DEAD, OR TO
BUSINESSES, COMPANIES, EVENTS, INSTITUTIONS, OR LO-
CALES IS COMPLETELY COINCIDENTAL.

SLENDERMAN/CONNIE MYRES.
1ST ED.

ISBN — 13: 978-1-957819-04-4 (E-BOOK)
ISBN — 13: 978-1-957819-05-1 (HARDCOVER)
ISBN — 13: 978-1-957819-06-8 (PAPERBACK)

*Dedicated to my family and friends, especially my sons
Lucas and Charles Kraus for their loyal support
and encouragement of all my projects.
I appreciate you.*

Contents

SLENDERMAN

Chapter 1

NINE-YEAR-OLD MORGAN RAFFERTY SAT the white plastic grocery bag filled with hot dog buns on top of the park's picnic table. She rubbed the goosebumps on her arms, wondering why her hairs prickled. It was not cold outside, in fact, it was a sweltering Saturday morning. It gave her a creepy feeling, like something bad was going to happen.

Morgan tucked a few strands of her long brown hair behind an ear. "When do we get to eat?"

"It won't be long," her mom, Mary said, setting the cooler next to the buns. "It'll take a little while for the coals to get hot. You can go play with the other kids, just don't wander off."

Morgan glanced at the dozen tables under the roof of the open pavilion. "Where's Jerome's birthday cake?"

"Cassandra's bringing it. She's waiting for Jerome to finish setting up his project at school so that it's ready for the science fair tomorrow." Mary watched the growing number of kids fill the park; some she recognized, like Jerome's grandparents and aunt and uncle, and others she did not. Then she saw Cassandra and Jerome get out of their car. "They're here now. I'm going to help them carry things for the party. I'll be right back."

"Let's go swing," Morgan said to her younger brother, Tyler.

"Okay," he said as he raced toward the swing set.

Sugar Sand Park in Black Water was Morgan's favorite place to play. Not only did it have swings but also a wooden fort to climb into and slide out of, a merry-go-round, and teeter-totters. There was even a path that led into the woods. She had walked the trail before with her dad. They would follow it to the fork; one way went to the beach and the other way led deeper into the dark mass of trees. They never went that way; she was not sure why. Maybe it was because of wild animals, or maybe they would get lost; he never really said. But going to the beach was the best choice anyway because there were sand dunes, smooth stones to toss in the water, and sugar sand to build castles with.

"I beat you," Tyler said, sitting on his favorite swing, one of the smaller ones that hung closer to the ground.

Morgan sat on one a few seats down and swung. Swinging too high was a little scary because the park sat on top of a hill and looked out over Lake Michigan. Sometimes it made her feel like she was on the roof of a skyscraper and if she would swing too high, she might fly off the seat and soar over the edge and out of sight, landing in a soft pile of sand or possibly be scooped up by a passing seagull where she would ride on its back like Harry Potter on a broom. Morgan knew that could not happen; she was fairly sure of it. Nevertheless, she gripped the chains so tight that her hands ached.

"Hey, guys," Jerome said, running up to them. He wiped the perspiration from his brow and sat down on a swing between the two of them. "Can you believe I'm eight years old now?"

"I'm older than you," Morgan said, slowing her swing. "I'm nine."

"I'll be eight next year," Tyler chimed in.

The sun was bright, and the air felt wet on the summer day. The wind gusting off the lake kept blowing Morgan's long hair over her eyes. She should have let her mom pull it back into a ponytail. The swing's arc was now a gentle undulation as Morgan looked over at the pavilion. There were lots of people, mostly kids running around, laughing, and screaming. "Do you know all these people, Jerome?"

Jerome looked around. "Nope, not all of them. I know Grammy and Gramps and Uncle James and Aunt Sue and all my cousins. I think there's a ton of people here for the science fair tomorrow."

Morgan was not sure of that logic. "Maybe. Or it could be because it's hot as hell and people want to go swimming."

"Awe, you just swore," Tyler said. "I'm telling mom."

"I'm just stating a fact." Morgan glared at Tyler. "Okay, it's hot as heck. Is that better?"

Jerome laughed as he rose to the skyscraper height.

Morgan dragged the toes of her shoes in the sand, bringing her swing to a stop. She stood up and walked toward the trail.

"Where are you going?" Tyler shouted.

"I saw a little bunny rabbit."

Tyler brought his swing to a stop. "You're not supposed to go in the woods without mom or dad."

"I'm not going in the woods," she shouted back.

"Looks like it to me," Tyler said.

Morgan stopped in front of the path. A cute little rabbit was nibbling on some grass along the trail's edge. She looked back at Tyler and Jerome who were watching her, then crossed the line from the mown lawn into the tree shadows. It was cooler than being out in the open and the wind was calm, calm enough for an annoying mosquito to buzz around her face. As Morgan approached the rabbit, it hopped farther down the path. She would take a couple of steps and it would take a couple of hops, drawing her deeper into the darkness.

Morgan was not afraid. She knew the fork was ahead and that if she did not go left, things would be fine. But the silly rabbit led her to the fork. She looked back, way back, and saw that Tyler and Jerome had followed her and were now standing at the cutoff point, the point between light and dark. They shouted at her to turn around, but the bunny was almost within her reach. When she caught it, she would take it back and show them the cute little animal. It would all be worth it.

Now at the fork in the path, she groaned. The bunny turned left, but it was so close. What would it hurt to go down the left fork and into the depth of the forest for just a little way? That is all she must do to catch the cuddly little thing. So she did.

Then she heard someone say, "I can get the bunny for you."

There before her was a tall man, taller than her dad and skinnier, way skinnier. He wore an old-fashioned black suit with a black tie, and when she looked at his face, she had difficulty telling if he was smiling at her because the gloomy shadows obscured its paleness. She knew she was not supposed to talk to strangers, but he must be someone important, someone who could be trusted because he was dressed up in a business-man's suit. She nodded.

The man reached down and picked up the rabbit. "I will give him to you if you come and get him."

Morgan watched him pet the bunny. It surprised her that it was not trying to jump out of his hands. She stood still. "Who are you?"

"I am no one to worry about, Morgan. I live down this trail in a palace where there are candy cane trees, cotton candy flowers, and a playhouse made of gingerbread. And I even have a little white pony that you could ride. Its mane is braided with pink ribbons and bows. Have you ever ridden a pony?"

Morgan was not sure she saw his mouth move when he spoke, or even if he had eyes. But it was dark, she reasoned. She nodded; she wanted to visit the magical place, but how did he know her name? "Do you know me?"

"Of course, I know you, Morgan." His voice was nonthreat-ening. "I am friends with your father. He speaks of you often. I have even been to your home, but I do not think you saw me. Your father would surely approve of you visiting me. You can trust me."

Morgan knew she should run away, run back to where Tyler and Jerome were, but there was a part of her that, to her surprise, was sure it was safe to go with this strange man.

The man extended the rabbit toward her. "You can come and get the cute little bunny, and then I will show you my magical home. I am sure you will enjoy it. Later, I will invite Tyler and Jerome to visit. That would be a lot of fun, don't you think?"

And so, Morgan did as the odd man said.

"Mom, mom!" Tyler yelled as he and Jerome sprinted to the pavilion.

Mary had just finished putting a sailboat adorned table-cloth on a picnic table. She looked up as she smoothed out the fold marks. "What's going on?"

Tyler was gasping for air. "A man took Morgan."

"A tall skinny man in the woods," Jerome said without hesitation.

Mary drew in a convulsive breath. "Where? Where is she?"

"On the trail, she was chasing a rabbit. I'll show you." Tyler waved for his mom to follow him as he raced back toward the trail in the woods.

Cassandra, who was standing next to Mary, was about to place the birthday cake on the clean tablecloth when it dropped from her hands, splattering on the concrete floor. "I'm calling the police," Cassandra shouted after them. Her trembling hands almost made it impossible to pull the phone from her back pocket.

"Morgan, where are you?" Mary cried out as she ran with the boys to the trail.

"She was down there." Tyler pointed toward where he had last seen Morgan. "Back by where the trail turns."

"Which way did she go?"

"She went left, that's where the man was."

Panicked, Mary trotted down the path as other parents ran up behind her. "Morgan, answer me. Where are you?"

One dad looked down the path and then back at the boys. "Are you sure she went that way? I don't see anyone."

"Tyler's right, the man took her that way," Jerome said. "I saw him. He was super tall, not fat at all, and wore clothes like the guy who buried my Grandpa Wilson."

Mary's breaths did not come easy. She stopped and looked at the boys. "You two, go back to the playground."

At least a dozen adults were now in the woods. Some followed the trail to the left, while others went right. Several parents scoured the forest outside the path, looking for any clues to the disappearance.

Then a horrifying scream pierced the desperate shouts for Morgan. There before Mary was a dead rabbit, its neck twisted in a way that made its head face backward. It lay motionless in the center of the trail so as not to be missed. Mary knew in her gut that the man did this gruesome act as a sign. A sign that he had Morgan and could do as he pleased.

Morgan was not found that day.

Chapter 2

PACIE ROSE STOOD UP in the lower garden and groaned as she brushed the soil from the knees of her blue jeans. She put her hands on her hips and stretched side to side as she looked up at the cloudless late afternoon azure sky and then back down at the June-bearing strawberry patch. "Next year I'm putting everything in raised beds. This bending over and crawling around on my hands and knees is getting old."

"First you have to build them," her daughter Amanda Booth said, putting strawberries into her half-full plastic bucket. "You should get Johnny to do it for you."

"He's pretty busy running the antique shop." Pacie paused, then said. "I can probably do it myself. I helped with a lot of the house renovations."

Ever since Pacie's husband, Patrick Rose, drowned in Lake Michigan several years ago, she has lived alone in her Black Water home—an 1879 British Palladian-style three-story mansion on the shore of Lake Michigan. A long-deceased ancestor who made his fortune building railroad cars built it. Fortunately for Pacie the home and land were paid off, and investment accounts from the family fortune paid the taxes.

Pacie lived in a small part of the three-story home. As finances and time allowed, she worked on renovating the nearly fifty rooms inside the Indiana limestone exterior. She and Patrick had done a lot of the improvements themselves, adding a kitchen, bathroom, and garage on the north side of the mansion. Fortunately, the slate blue roof and cupola were finished before he vanished, preventing further water damage.

Johnathon Armstrong, the owner of Good Old Days Antique Shop, became her significant other. She knows he wants to marry her, he has said so, but she just cannot cross that bridge. Not yet, anyway. Although presumed dead, the body of her husband has never been found. What if he came back? What if mobsters had taken him and he is still alive somewhere? He did work as a detective and most certainly gained enemies along the way. The authorities said that a rip current had pulled him under the water and away from the shore; but because Patrick was an expert swimmer and familiar with the Great Lakes, she had difficulty believing that explanation. Without a body, there was a tiny bit of doubt in Pacie's mind.

"I can help make the raised beds, Grandma. I want to keep having the yummy jam every year," Charlotte said. She looked at her mom, Amanda. "I know what we can do. Next year you and I can pick the strawberries and grandma and Irma can make the jam."

"I don't have a problem with that," Amanda said. "We just have to get our cousin Irma away from that police scanner and stop finding investigations for her and mom to do."

Charlotte laughed. "Yeah, she's a gray-haired old lady who

acts like a little kid. A little kid obsessed with Black Water's weirdness. And with being Grandma's sidekick."

"It's not nice to talk about people behind their back," Amanda said. "Even with all her quirks, she has helped the people of Black Water. Without Mom and Irma, we would never have found out what caused that virus to spread around town a while back."

Charlotte laughed. "I remember we helped them disguise themselves as janitors so that they could snoop around the hospital and figure out what was going on. It was fun finding wigs and janitor clothes from the secondhand store."

"Ah yes, I remember that. We were almost recognized, but Irma faked a minor medical problem, and we were able to get out of there before they escorted us to the emergency room— or to a waiting police car," Pacie said, rubbing her aching neck. "As far as Irma, her heart is in the right place."

Pacie enjoyed these times when her family came over and they worked on a project. Today it was both canning and freezing strawberry jam. This fall everyone will come to her pumpkin patch and pick out their own pumpkins and carve them. And soon after that, it will be making Christmas wreaths to hang on front doors.

Black Water, Michigan, was the perfect town to live in, not too big, not too small. As a resort town on the shore of Lake Michigan, it had much to offer—a lighthouse, sandy beaches and dunes, quaint downtown shops, and homes with yards large enough to grow those darned strawberries.

Pacie's phone rang. She pulled it from her pocket and looked at the number. "Hi, Irma, what's up?"

"I have another case for us. I'm a little late on this, but I heard on the police scanner that a child was abducted from Sugar Sand Park earlier today. The description two other kids gave the cops was that some tall creepy guy in a suit snatched her."

"A tall, creepy guy? When is Black Water going to stop having so many strange problems?"

"I don't know." Irma coughed. "But I still say it's the nuclear power plant causing it. As soon as they began building that thing outside of town in the late nineteen-sixties, weird things began happening. You know that."

"I know. But weird things have been happening in this area for a long time before that. I think the Bulwark Nuclear Power Plant just made it worse."

"So, can we do it?"

Pacie looked at her family, quietly picking strawberries. She could tell they were listening to her conversation. She watched her red-headed granddaughter pop a ruby red strawberry into her mouth. Now old enough to drive, she hoped Charlotte was wise enough to not fall victim to a child abductor. But wise did not always have much to do with it; these psychos were cunning. God forbid it could ever happen to Char.

"You know I have a soft spot for kids—and the creepy." Pacie paused. "Let's do it." She heard her daughter say: not again.

Irma squealed like a child who had just been handed a wrapped gift to open. "I know the kidnapping happened earlier this morning, but we should head over there soon. Haley might still be there. You know she helps us, at least sometimes."

"I'm on my way." Pacie disconnected the call.

"What is it this time?" Amanda asked.

"A child has been abducted."

"Who?"

"I don't know the details. I'm heading over to Sugar Sand Park." Pacie watched Amanda and Charlotte put down their buckets. "Can you guys finish up here?"

"Not a problem," Amanda said. "By the time you get back, we should have the jam made."

"Can't wait," Pacie said, noticing the bright blue sky now looked dull, and the air was no longer crisp. It felt as though the air was a sponge, pulling in and squeezing out any surrounding moisture. She walked from the lower garden, through the circle driveway—past a sundial that sat in the center of the circular patch of grass—and toward the side door that entered the butler's pantry and finally into the study.

When Pacie got inside, she washed the red stain of strawberries from her hands and slung her satchel over a shoulder. Inside she kept a handheld voice recorder, small notebook, pens, flashlight, Swiss army knife, and more.

As glorious as living in a mansion was, one of its drawbacks was the long walks to get anywhere. Pacie spent most of her time in the north end of the mansion where her study and the additions were built. Even her bedroom was easily accessed by a secondary staircase off of the study that allowed easy access to the second floor and the master suite. She lifted the car keys from the hook in the kitchen by the door leading into the garage.

A feeling of dread was making a subtle entrance into her chest as she climbed into the silver SUV. An image of a tall, creepy guy entered her mind as she drove down the driveway and onto the street. He would be fairly easy to spot, but she could think of no one who matched that description. Strike that, she could think of a couple of tall creepy guys, but they were not child abductors. One was the high school principal, who has lived in Black Water all his life, and the other was the undertaker in town. The only one of those two that wore a suit was Adam Cully, and she had a hard time believing this family man who has been the director at Black Water's funeral home for years could do such a thing. It made no sense.

Several minutes later, Pacie pulled into the parking lot behind Good Old Days Antique Shop. She smiled when she saw Johnny's pickup parked near the backdoor. She was not there to visit him, but instead to pick up Irma, who lived in the apartment above it. Irma was coming out of the first-floor door with her backpack. Pacie drove up to her.

"I'm sorry I pulled you from the garden, but I thought this was more important," Irma said as she climbed into the vehicle. The portable scanner was squawking from inside her pack.

"You're right, this is more important than some strawberries," Pacie said. Then she saw Johnny walk out of the shop's backdoor and toss a trash bag into the dumpster. She rolled down her window and waved.

Johnny walked over to the car and leaned on the door. "What are you ladies up to today?"

"We have a new case," Irma said right away. "We need to stop the tall creepy guy who's abducting kids."

"I heard that on the radio." He smiled at Pacie. "I think I know the answer, but do you have time to grab something to eat?"

"No, we're already running late. We have to get over to the park and see what's going on before everyone leaves."

Johnny kissed Pacie, then whispered in her ear, "I miss you."

His breath felt warm on her skin. She did not want to leave. "I'll call you later when I find out more."

"You ladies be careful," he said, backing away from the car. "Don't forget to let the police do the dirty work."

Pacie waved goodbye and drove out of the lot. One reason they had good luck solving cases was that, as citizen reporters, they did things they were not supposed to do, like sneaking into places important to the case. Johnny did not know all their shenanigans. Pacie told him about some of the more innocent mischiefs that they got themselves into, but the more questionable details were better left unsaid.

When they arrived at Sugar Sand Park, what appeared to be search team members were walking out of the woods, past the empty playground, toward the parking lot where police officers and reporters were gathered.

"There's Haley," Irma said, vigorously waving her arms as she got out of the car.

"I think she saw you," Pacie said, putting her satchel cross-body as she sized up the situation.

"She's coming," Irma said. She switched off the police scanner before taking her handheld video camera from the backpack.

"Hi, ladies," Detective Haley Wanat said, approaching

them. "I'm not surprised to see you here, but you are a little late to this crime scene. They're just finishing up the grid search for this area."

"Good to see you, Detective," Pacie said, extending a hand. "I hear a child was kidnapped. Are you able to tell us anything?"

Pacie's husband was Det. Wanat's partner. The presumed death of Patrick was almost as hard on Haley as it was on Pacie. Ever since Det. Wanat delivered the eulogy at Patrick's funeral, Pacie and Det. Wanat had become good friends. Even though they were on a first-name basis, Pacie addressed her formally in public. Mostly because Haley would tell them more information about cases than she should, and Pacie did not want to get her friend into trouble. It was an unspoken agreement that both Irma and she would never reveal their source. For that reason, Irma turned on her camera and began recording with it facing the ground, capturing their feet. Onlookers did not need to know what they were talking about. Sometimes Pacie would slip a hand into her satchel and turn on her recorder without witnesses knowing. For all anyone knew, the three of them were talking about the weather.

"A nine-year-old girl, Morgan Rafferty, was abducted. The woman talking to the officer over there is her mother, Mary, and the little boy is her brother, Tyler. Tyler, and the other boy, Jerome Cushing, standing by that car with his mom, Cassandra, are both witnesses. The boys saw the perp, albeit from a distance."

"What did they see?" Pacie asked, watching Irma step closer to the detective.

"Their stories are the same. They were here for Jerome's

birthday party and went to play on the swings. Then Morgan saw a rabbit hopping around on the trail that goes into the woods. All three kids knew they were not supposed to follow the trail into the forest without a parent, but Morgan insisted on following the rabbit. The boys went to the trail and stood at its mouth, watching Morgan. That's when, and this gets kind of weird, they saw a tall man, around eight to ten feet tall, appear on the trail leading deeper into the forest."

"Appear? Was he walking from a certain direction?"

"Apparently, the perp was suddenly there." Detective Wanat looked around, then said, "Not only was he really tall, like Bigfoot, as one of the boys said—"

"That's right," Irma interrupted. "Bigfoots are that tall. Did it look like Bigfoot?"

"No, it looked like an extremely thin man. He wore an old-fashioned black suit with a tie, like the guy who buried Jerome's grandfather, they said."

"Did they recognize him as someone from town?" Pacie asked.

"No, they said his face was colored like white milk and they could not see eyes, a nose, or a mouth. And one boy said there appeared to be octopus arms coming from behind it. Doesn't sound like anyone I know."

"Sounds kinda spooky," Pacie said. "Do you have a description for the little girl?"

"Morgan Rafferty was last seen wearing a white blouse and shorts. She has long dark hair with loose waves and of average weight and height for a nine-year-old."

"Did you find any physical clues?" Irma asked.

"Not yet. People from the park began searching almost immediately, but it was like the girl and the man just disappeared. I take that back. There was a dead rabbit, probably the one the girl was chasing, lying in the middle of the trail with its head twisted around. Likely done by the perp as a show of power and control."

Pacie saw the moms and kids getting into their cars, sobbing. "I don't think they're up to an interview."

"I doubt it. Besides, I just told you everything they told me. We've been searching the area by land, air, and water. And we have a bulletin out. Keep your eyes open because abductors often return to assist in the search," Det. Wanat said. "The team will search extensively for a few days."

"Why do kidnappers do that?" Irma asked.

"They often want to monitor the progress of the case and to mislead the search effort," Det. Wanat said. She turned when she heard Officer Branden Kline call her name. "Gotta go. You two be careful, I don't think we're dealing with an ordinary man."

"Do you need help with the search?" Pacie asked.

"We have it covered," the detective said, walking away.

Pacie's shoulder muscles tightened. "I've seen no one that matches that strange description around town."

Irma turned off her camera. "Me either. It has to be someone new to Black Water."

Pacie and Irma walked toward the pavilion as officers finished barricading the trail with yellow tape, telling the curious—like Pacie and Irma—POLICE LINE DO NOT CROSS.

"Everyone's leaving," Irma said as they walked into the pavilion where birds were pecking away at the spilled cake on the dirty cement floor. Paper plates, cups, and other trash were scattered around, indicating people were in a rush to leave a chaotic scene.

"When we're alone, we'll check out the trail before it gets dark," Pacie said. She stood there listening. She heard the waves along the beach, a crow's harsh caw, and the clanking of swings banging into each other from the wind. No screams or cries for help.

Irma was video recording the park as Pacie walked toward the swings. She felt so bad for the little girl. Where was she and, more importantly, was she alright?

"It sure is humid," Irma said, momentarily pulling the fabric of her flowered blouse away from her skin.

Pacie looked back at the parking lot and saw the last patrol car pull out. "They're gone. Let's check out the trail."

They walked up to the police tape and stopped. When they were sure no one was watching, they ducked under it and walked into the cool dimness of the forest's edge. Pacie slowly walked down the path, looking around for anything out of the ordinary.

"I see lots of footprints," Irma said, still recording. Vague indents in the sand of varying sizes showed a well-traveled path. "None look like Bigfoot, though."

"I've never heard of Bigfoot wearing a suit."

"I'm just saying." Irma stopped recording and walked next to Pacie. "What are you thinking?"

Pacie took her cellphone from her back pocket. "My

battery is at ninety-eight percent."

"Are you going to call someone?"

"No, well maybe, if I have to call nine-one-one." She put the phone back in her pocket.

When they reached the fork in the trail, they stopped.

"Where's the dead rabbit?" Irma asked.

"I think that way," Pacie said, pointing to the left. "Haley said the guy was on the path that went deeper into the forest. The other way goes to the beach."

"I wonder if we should split up?" Irma said, looking down the path that led to the lake.

"The guy is probably already gone, especially since the area has already been searched." Pacie began walking down the left fork.

"I changed my mind; I'm going with you." Irma followed behind Pacie as they ventured deeper into the thick trees. She stopped when a loud snap of wood came from the forest floor, about thirty yards away. She whispered, "What was that? It sounded heavy."

Pacie stopped, too. She looked in the sound's direction but saw nothing. "A deer, maybe."

"Or the guy," Irma said, raising her camera in the sound's direction. She zoomed in and then sighed with relief. "You're right, it's a deer."

The white-tailed deer bounded away.

Pacie looked back at the trail entrance. "I don't think the boys can see much farther than this, so the little girl must have been abducted in this area."

"Do you see the rabbit?" Irma asked.

"There it is", Pacie said, pointing just off the trail where it had been pushed aside.

They walked up to it and bent over to take a closer look.

"Poor little thing," Irma said, snapping a shot.

Pacie took her phone and looked up a map of the area. "This trail doesn't go out to a road for what looks like several miles. It seems to go to a river that runs behind the power plant and then stops. It picks up again further away."

Irma looked up at the sky through tree boughs. "It's getting cloudy, I wonder if it's going to rain."

"Rain isn't in the forecast," Pacie said. "Let's keep going before we run out of daylight."

And so they did. It grew darker the deeper into the forest they went. Up and down hills for over an hour. Then they reached an eight-foot-high chain-link security fence that kept them from going any farther.

"I guess this is the end of the line," Pacie said, looking through the steel wire mesh of the fence. "You can tell the trail used to cross that river, probably before Bulwark was built."

"Yeah, and there's no way that guy could've crossed here because it would be impossible to get over the fence," Irma said, looking up at the three strands of barbed wire that ran along its top. "But he *was* ten feet tall."

Pacie looked at her phone again. "I don't know how accurate this map is, but there aren't any nearby roads that a car can travel, other than what leads to the power plant. So where did they go?"

"I don't know."

Pacie looked left and right along the boundary. "There's

no footpath along this side of the fence so if they followed it, it would've been tough going with all those prickly raspberry bushes."

"There's no sign of anything being disturbed," Irma said. She looked at the hills around them and the backside of a dune. Past the treetops, foggy clouds of steam billowed from the nuclear power plant's cooling towers. "It's as though the ground swallowed them up."

Chapter 3

"LET'S HEAD BACK," PACIE said, turning around. "I don't want to be out here in the dark."

"Any ideas on who you think it is?"

Pacie shrugged. "No, I don't."

"But what about how the kids described him—ten feet tall, no face, and stuff?"

"I don't think they were lying," Pacie said. "They must have misinterpreted what they saw; they weren't that close to it."

"It? You said *it*." Irma was excited. "What else are you thinking?"

"Well, if what they were seeing is correct, then it's not a normal human."

"If not Bigfoot, then what?"

"I don't know." Pacie looked around. She had the uneasy feeling that someone was watching them. "But I'm sure it's not Bigfoot. It could be someone with that hormone disease that makes them extremely tall. I think it's called gigantism."

"And no face?" Irma said. "Maybe it's an alien. That's a possibility."

"We have no tangible evidence yet, only eyewitness accounts."

They crested a hill and began walking down into a damp gully before climbing the hill on the other side. The mosquitoes were thick and deer flies were being their usual aggressive selves. They swatted the biting insects as they landed on the top of their heads.

"Quiet." Pacie focused on an area in the thickets.

"What?" Irma whispered, trying to swat the bugs as quietly as she could off her shoulders.

Pacie saw movement from a dense group of bushes. She whispered and pointed. "Focus your camera over there, about thirty or forty yards away. I saw something."

Irma focused her camera where Pacie was pointing. She zoomed in as a mosquito landed on her hand. "I smell something awful, but I'm not seeing anything yet."

Pacie felt like she was in a Bigfoot video where someone claims to see the creature. But all the camera picks up are shadows, blurs, and something that might be in the shape of a bulky body. "Do you see anything?"

Deer flies bit Irma in the part of her hair and the side of her face. She smacked them, causing the camera to lose its focus. "I can't take this, Pacie. I've got to get out of here."

"No problem," Pacie said, turning on her phone's flashlight.

Pacie and Irma ran up the hill and as far down the trail as they could until they had to stop and rest. While they caught their breath, they could see subdued light spilling in from the open yard of the park farther down the trail.

"Did you see something with your camera?" Pacie asked.

"No, it was too dark. Did you see something?"

"No. I guess we just freaked ourselves out."

They laughed as they began walking toward the fork. When they reached it, they turned and look back where they had run from.

"I don't think I'm ever walking back down there again," Irma said.

"Come on," Pacie said, jogging down the trail toward the entrance. "Let's record the video for the website and think about what we have so far."

"So far, not so much," Irma said, keeping pace behind her.

They ran out of the woods and into the diminishing sunlight, still trying to scorch the landscape.

"I don't know what's worse," Pacie said, wiping her brow. "Being in there with the biting bugs or out here in this heat."

"Being in there with the bugs," Irma said. "Plus, there's no monster lurking out in the open."

"That we know of," Pacie said, grinning.

Irma held up her camera and turned on the light. "Stand in front of the trail so that we have it as a backdrop."

Pacie ran her fingers through her hair, trying to look more presentable for the camera. She never enjoyed making the videos, but thanks to Irma's prodding, and the community's need to know about any danger that could befall them, Pacie learned to *almost* enjoy it.

"I'm ready if you're ready," Irma said, bringing Pacie into focus.

Pacie cleared her throat. "I'm Pacie Rose, citizen reporter here at Sugar Sand Park in Black Water, Michigan. It is late

Saturday, June fourteenth. A nine-year-old girl was abducted while walking on the trail behind me. The eyewitnesses describe the perpetrator as being an extremely tall, skinny man wearing a black suit with a tie. If you know about the incident or have seen anyone matching the description, please contact the authorities. This is Pacie Rose, citizen reporter. Stay tuned for further updates."

"It was short, but it'll work for now," Irma said, putting the camera into her backpack. "I'll get this uploaded to the site and let the paper and WBLA know we have a video ready."

"Sounds good," Pacie said, walking toward the car. "The town has such trust in me. I hope I don't let them down."

"You haven't yet. Besides, they love you and want to see your take on these situations. The news reporters do a superb job, but it's the personal investment that you put into the research we do that makes the paper and the TV station keep using our stuff as a supplement."

"Or filler." Pacie looked at her watch; Johnny would be closing the shop soon. "I'm giving Johnny a call."

"Hey, babe," Johnny said. "Are you done for the day?"

Pacie unlocked the SUV. "Yep. I'm heading over there now."

"Great, I'll see you in a bit."

Pacie and Irma got into the car. Pacie looked out over the empty playground. "It's so strange seeing that police tape here."

"I'll be on the lookout for someone matching the tall creepy guy description," Irma said, looking toward the woods.

"Don't go down that trail alone," Pacie said, backing out of her parking spot. "I get the feeling this guy would harm adults, too."

"I don't think you have to worry about that," Irma said.

As they drove to the antique shop, they could not help but scan every sidewalk, every yard, and every alley for someone who matched the crazed man's description.

"Everyone I'm seeing looks normal," Pacie said.

"The paper has a picture of the nine-year-old girl." Irma held up her phone for Pacie to see. "I'll email it to you."

"We need to find her fast before it's too late," Pacie said, slowing for a stop sign. "I heard that seventy-four percent of abducted children who are ultimately murdered are dead within three hours of the abduction. And we're past that window."

"So, what's the plan?"

Pacie drove into the downtown parking lot behind the shop and parked near Johnny's pickup truck, complete with a cap over the bed so that he can easily hall the antiques he collects. "Besides scouring Black Water for the perp and the little girl, and asking a lot of questions? I'm not sure."

Irma opened her car door. "I'll be in my apartment."

"And I'll be talking to Johnny."

They got out of the car. Irma went into the building's backdoor leading to one of two apartments above Good Old Days Antique Shop. The second-floor apartment belonged to Irma, and the third and final floor apartment was Johnny's.

The shop door's antique shopkeeper's bell jingled as Pacie walked in the backdoor. She walked down the short hallway, flanked to the right with three doors: one leading to the basement, another to a storage room, and the third was another way to reach the staircase leading to the apartments. She saw

Johnny speaking with an elderly couple who appeared to be interested in an antique hand mirror and brush.

Pacie loved walking around the antiques in the shop. Rather than being a hodgepodge of furniture, toys, and books, he had items organized by room. She walked into her favorite room, the library. To the right was a decorative walnut bookcase where Johnny kept the latest books that he would add to the various collections. She browsed through the fragile hardcovers, but as much as she enjoyed looking at them, she was not a fan of really old things. It seemed to her that there was too much history connected to them. It felt as though they held the memories of other people who they had once belonged to; the people who once held them and kept them close by. But that was her. She knew it was silly. Nevertheless, it bothered her. Johnny would sometimes joke with her about items being haunted, especially old dolls. But truth be told, some items *did* bother him, but he rarely admitted it. On more than a few occasions, he admitted to being relieved when certain items had sold and were no longer in the shop. One such item was a doll from the late eighteen-hundreds. Its bisque doll head had cracks scattered over its face. Johnny said that it seemed to walk around the shop when it was closed, and no one was around. When he opened the shop in the morning, he would find it in another location. At first, he thought Irma was coming downstairs and playing a prank on him, but she always denied it. Pacie remembered him being so unnerved by the events that he sold the doll at a loss to a collector in town; he did not want to take the chance that a parent would come in and buy it for their child. He called the doll Jezebel, the bad girl.

Pacie heard goodbyes echoed and saw the couple leave with the carefully wrapped antique mirror and brush in hand. The decorative clock near the counter said eight o'clock. Johnny turned off the open sign and walked to Pacie. He embraced her and kissed her on the lips. "Are you hungry?"

"I'm starving."

"I have some leftovers upstairs that I can heat for us, if that's alright."

At first, she thought he was going to take her out to a restaurant. "Sounds good."

"Great." Johnny locked the exterior doors and grabbed a set of keys from under the counter. Then he opened the door leading to the staircase and motioned with his hand. "After you, my lady."

The automatic motion sensor light turned on as they walked into a small foyer. Inside was an elevator and the stair-case near the door Irma had used to enter the building. "When are you going to get that old elevator fixed?"

"One of these days," Johnny said, making sure the other exterior door was locked. "Actually, it does work; I just don't trust it until it's been inspected. And it's past due for an inspection."

The wooden stairs creaked as they ascended. They passed the landing to Irma's apartment, complete with a brown welcome mat on the floor and a wreath made of seashells on the door. It was the wreath Irma had made during their first day of a spring party at Pacie's house.

"Did your cousin come home with you?"

"Yeah, she's in there."

They climbed one more level to Johnny's nondescript landing. He unlocked the door, and they walked inside. The two apartments were large, both with open floor plans. Three large, tall windows faced the downtown street. The woodwork and hardwood floors were original, but the kitchen, bath, pipes, and electrical wiring had been updated a few years ago.

Johnny took a bottle of Sauvignon Blanc—tastes of juicy citrus and the scent of fresh-cut lemongrass—from the built-in wine rack and uncorked it.

"I have to drive home," Pacie said. "Do you have iced tea or something with no alcohol?"

Johnny poured two glasses of the light green wine. "You have no excuse. You live alone and you don't have any pets to tend to like Irma does. And speaking of Irma, she's darn lucky because she's the only person I'll let have pets here."

Pacie smiled and took the glass he handed her and sat on a stool at the bar. She took her notepad from her satchel. "All she has is a cute little Staffie."

"Mr. Dibble is so ugly he's cute." Johnny took a casserole pan covered in foil from the refrigerator. "Does a hamburger and noodle casserole sound good?"

"Sounds tasty," Pacie said, jotting down notes about the case.

Johnny spooned some casserole onto a plate and put it into the microwave. "So you're working on an abduction case?"

"Yeah, a nine-year-old girl named Morgan Rafferty was abducted at Sugar Sand Park this morning by some super tall, skinny guy in a black suit."

"A tall and skinny guy in a suit could be a lot of people."

"You're right, but it gets weird."

"Your cases are always weird."

Pacie nodded. "The kids who saw him said he was as tall as Bigfoot, which means around seven to ten feet tall. And they said he had pale skin with no eyes, nose, or mouth."

The microwave dinged. Johnny took out the dish and placed it in front of Pacie. He put another plate in the microwave. He handed Pacie a fork. "You're right, that's weird. It doesn't sound like anyone I know." He laughed.

"That's what we all said."

"I'm sorry, I didn't mean to laugh; this whole thing is awful. I'll keep an eye out for a strange slender man roaming around town."

"Hmm, slender man. That sounds vaguely familiar." She took a bite of the beef and noodles. "This is good. Did you make it from scratch?"

"Surprised it's not Hamburger Helper?"

"Actually, yeah."

"I'm disappointed that you have little faith in my culinary skills," Johnny said. He took his heated food from the microwave and sat down next to Pacie.

"I'm joking, you're actually a very good cook."

"So what's your next move?"

"I'm not sure. We did a video; Irma is probably processing it now." Pacie took her phone from her pocket and found the picture that Irma had sent her. "Here's a picture of the little girl."

"She's pretty. Send me her picture and I'll watch for her."

They chatted about the heatwave, going to the beach, all while avoiding further talk of the abduction as they finished their food and moved to the living room couch.

"Another glass of wine?"

"No, I have to get back home. Mandy and Char were going to finish picking the strawberries and make jam. I just need to make sure they locked the house door, and that nothing was left out to spoil." Pacie looked at her watch. "It's getting late. I should probably leave now."

Johnny ran a hand along Pacie's cheek. "You're beautiful, Pacie."

She smiled. "You're wonderful, Johnny."

"Wonderful? That's all I am is wonderful," Johnny teased, pulling her close.

"Sorry, I didn't mean it that way. I love you, Johnny." And Pacie meant it.

They smooched until Johnny said, "Pacie, you'd better leave now before I refuse to let you go. I'm getting a little hot and bothered." And Johnny meant it.

Pacie laughed, then whispered in his ear, "One of these days, my dear prince, we will be united. Together for eternity."

"If you're leaving, you'd better do it now," Johnny said, keeping her close to his body.

Pacie backed away, and when he finally loosened his hold on her, she stood up. "I'm not saying I *want* to leave."

"You don't need to explain, I understand." Johnny stood and walked her to the door. "Call me if you need anything. It worries me that some psycho is running around town and you live there in that big old mansion all alone. Not to mention all the doors for an intruder to try and break in through."

"Don't worry, I will. Besides, I check the doors periodically and make sure they're locked." Pacie kissed him and opened the door. "Oh, and thanks for the leftovers."

"Not a problem. Anytime you get a hankering for a micro-waved casserole, you know where to go." Johnny took his keys from a not-so-old glass ashtray he kept near the door. "I'll walk you out."

Johnny walked behind her down the old creaky steps. When they reached the bottom landing, Pacie stepped aside so that he could unlock the door. They walked into the off-white lights of the parking lot. "It feels muggy out here."

"It's been muggy all day," Pacie said, walking next to him in the light's quietness. "I haven't been in the luxury of air conditioning all day like some people I know."

"Do you really think it's fun staying indoors all day in the nice cool temperature?" Johnny nudged her with his elbow.

"Days like today? Yes." She unlocked her car and opened the door. "I'll call you tomorrow."

Johnny kissed her. "I'll talk to you then. Drive careful."

"I will," Pacie said, slipping into the SUV. She turned on the ignition and watched Johnny walk to the backdoor. He looked back over his shoulder and waved as Pacie drove from the parking spot. She waved back and rolled down her window as she drove onto the street. She wanted to hear sounds, sounds like someone in distress, as she drove slowly home. Several minutes later, she pulled into her driveway without hearing or seeing anything abnormal. She clicked the garage door opener as she drove up to her house. The windows were dark; no one was there. She veered to the right and pulled into the garage, closing the door behind her.

Nervous from the events of the day, Pacie hurried to the house door and tested it. They locked it. Not that she did not trust Mandy and Charlotte to lock the doors, it was that she wanted to be absolutely sure no one had entered her home while she was away. She had this fear that someone could be hiding in her closet, or God forbid, under her bed. Not to mention the 49 rooms most of which she did not enter. Totally irrational, of course.

Chapter 4

IRMA UPLOADED THE VIDEO they had taken at the park to both YouTube and their website. There they not only posted videos but articles and pictures of the cases they had done. It was a lot of work, but Irma enjoyed maintaining it.

"I wonder if the camera picked up something that I didn't see." With her camera still connected to the computer, she scanned through the extra clips until she came to the one where they were in the gully on the trail and Pacie wanted her to zoom in on something. Frame by frame, she began going through it. Then something caught her attention. It was a shadow, a dark black shadow, darker than what surrounded it, near a tree trunk. She heard herself say something stunk.

"What is that?" Irma said, zooming in on the figure. It looked like a man, a tall, thin man. It would move behind the tree trunk and then poke out its head and body as if it were watching them. Irma shivered. There really was someone watching them. Was it the kidnapper or just some guy walking in the woods? Maybe someone from the search party, but why didn't he say anything.

Irma looked at the clock. It was late enough that she thought Pacie was sleeping; she would call in the morning. She did a few screen grabs and emailed them to Pacie and Det. Wanat.

Mr. Dibble whimpered. Irma turned around and saw the Staffordshire Terrier standing at the door. "Do you need to go out, Mr. Dibble?"

Irma grabbed a flashlight, the keys, and then put the leash on the prancing dog.

"Let's go," Irma said, walking out of the apartment. They walked down the steps and out the door to the parking lot. She did not want to travel far from the building because what she saw on the video made her think someone could be stalking her, but she had no choice, Mr. Dibble needed grass.

Every sound made her jump—the slamming of a distant car door, something rummaging through the dumpster, even the sound of her footsteps. If that figure in the video was that creep, then where was the little girl. Dead? That would be what the statistics say. She doubted he would want to take a wrinkled old woman like herself, but who knew how this pervert thought.

"At least I have you, Mr. Dibble, to protect me. People see your muscles and they cower in fear," Irma said to the dog. "But I know you're just a cuddly little baby."

When they reached the large strip of grass that followed the sidewalk that ran along Inky River, Mr. Dibble sniffed every tree, trying to decide where to do his business. Mr. Dibble led Irma toward the lake.

Irma stopped walking when she heard shuffling behind

nearby bushes. Was it the kidnapper or someone watching her? More than likely it was a cat, or squirrels foraging for nuts or berries. Nevertheless, the sound gave her the chills, especially since Mr. Dibble was interested in it and tugged on the leash, wanting to investigate it.

"This is far enough, Mr. Dibble." She gave a gentle tug on the leash and began walking back to the apartment. The Staffie trotted alongside her until he finally found the proper spot to urinate.

"Took you long enough." Irma looked back at the bush from where the noise had come and saw a cat walking down the sidewalk. Relieved no one was watching her, she and Mr. Dibble rushed back to the building.

Irma went inside and tested the exterior door after she locked it. It was secure. As she and Mr. Dibble walked up the steps, she realized she had never taken her cellphone with her. What if she had needed to call for help? She would have to stop being so careless.

Mr. Dibble was first through the apartment door. Irma unhooked his leash. The pooch lapped water from his bowl and then proceeded to the couch where he curled up in a ball, ready for sleep. Irma patted his head and went back to her computer. Pacie had not replied to the pictures she emailed earlier. She yawned. "I'd better go to bed, but I don't want to.

Irma had a sleep study scheduled at Black Water General Hospital in a couple of days. She had recently begun sleepwalking, something she had never done before. The first night she woke up in the living room, sitting in her computer chair at her desk. The computer monitor was on a strange website that cycled through images of numbers, symbols, and dead animals. It horrified her. Then another night she woke up early because her feet felt cold and wet. When she looked at them, they were muddy with pieces of grass clippings attached. She thought it was from going barefoot at the beach earlier in the day, but it was too fresh. When she got out of bed to wash her feet, she saw the apartment door wide open. This was proof she had sleepwalked and had in fact left the building.

Terrified by the events, Irma made an appointment with Dr. Plum. He did a neurological exam and suggested the sleep study; he said it would help diagnose a sleep disorder. He thought it was possibly a condition where a person physically acts out vivid, unpleasant dreams. A dream-enacting behavior, the doctor said.

Irma had told Pacie none of this for two reasons. One, she did not want to concern Pacie with her problems, and two, she kept forgetting. But after more thought, she wanted Pacie to know and to go with her to the sleep study appointment. She wrote on a sticky note to call Pacie about it in the morning and stuck it on her desk calendar.

But now it was time for bed. Irma feared what could happen if she fell asleep. If she forced herself to stay awake all night, she would want to sleep during the day tomorrow and there was too much work to do on the recent case. Just because it happened before does not mean it would happen again, she reasoned, but she would need to take safety measures.

Irma put on her best pajamas just in case she was found wandering around outside. It was kind of like wearing clean underpants with no holes in them so as not to be embarrassed if someone were to see them if she were in an accident. She brushed her teeth and made sure the front door and windows were latched. Then she turned the air conditioning down a couple of degrees cooler and went into her bedroom; Mr. Dibble was at her heels.

Irma closed the bedroom door and locked it. "It's a little ridiculous to lock all this stuff, don't you think, Mr. Dibble? After all, I know how to unlock them. I need one of those pads that they put on a confused patient's bed in nursing homes that alert staff with an alarm if they were to try to get out of bed. That way the alarm should wake me up before I do something stupid."

"Ready for bed, Mr. Dibble?" She turned off the bedroom light and climbed into bed. Mr. Dibble jumped up next to her. With only a light sheet over her body, she closed her eyes.

One thing that Irma did not reveal totally to the doctor was about the nightmares she had been having. She told him she had been having bad dreams, but she did not mention the man. He would speak to her and tell her awful things, and things that she should do for him. If she carried out these grievous acts, he would reward her with riches beyond imagination, and a luxurious room in his palace. Mentioning these things would make her sound crazy. Mentioning thoughts of murder would buy her a locked room on the psychiatric floor of Black Water General.

Chapter 5

IT WAS ALMOST MIDNIGHT when Christine Jameson parked in her driveway where muted streetlights cast a dull light. She took her wallet from the glove compartment and placed it in her work bag next to a pair of safety glasses, gloves, and a box-cutter. She picked up the grimy bag from the passenger seat and carried it into her Black Water home. The air was sticky outside and even more so on the inside. She sat down on the bench near the door and took off her steel-toe work boots and sweat-soaked socks.

"That feels better", she said, wiggling her toes that were wrinkled like prunes.

The house was quiet as she walked into the kitchen. Her fourteen-year-old daughter Dora must have made a salad before going to bed because chopped pieces of onion and celery were scattered on the cutting board next to a chef's knife. After drinking a partial bottle of cold water from the refrigerator, she went into the bathroom and turned on the shower.

While in the shower, she heard the bathroom door open. "Is that you, Dora?"

There was no answer. Christine moved the shower curtain enough to peer out. The door was open, but no one was there. Dora must have wanted to use the bathroom and then changed her mind. Christine doubted her daughter had anyone spending the night because she would have told her.

After drying off, Christine donned a light cotton pajama top and shorts. Even with the bathroom window open, steam lingered in the air longer than usual. She quickly left the sauna and went upstairs to check on Dora, guided by nightlights to her daughter's room. The bedroom door was open, allowing the light to spill into the hallway.

"Dora, are you awake," Christine said as she nuzzled the door the rest of the way open. A journal lay on her unmade bed, but Dora was not in the room. Christine was surprised she had not seen her daughter. Normally if Dora was awake when she got home from work, she would have been greeted at some point before she went to bed.

Christine wanted to find Dora and say goodnight before falling asleep. She walked back down the hall and stood at the top of the steps, listening for a sound that would tell her where Dora was. Other than the tick of a clock, it was silent. She looked down the staircase into the darkness, now worried that Dora might not be in the house. But she had to be there because someone had opened the bathroom door while she was taking a shower.

"Dora, are you here?" Christine turned on the bright staircase light and walked downstairs. The television was turned off in the living room and Dora was not sleeping on the couch.

She walked to the kitchen and switched on the overhead

light. Dora was not there, either. Christine turned off the light and then back on. She looked at the cutting board. The knife was missing. Now she was paralyzed with fear; someone was in the house, and it was likely not Dora.

Then Christine heard a scratchy squealing sound coming from the downstairs office. It sounded like the computer was malfunctioning. She turned and looked down the hallway, past the bathroom, toward the office. The door was to the left, so she could not see inside. She would need to walk down there. But first, she needed her cellphone because something was wrong. More than likely there was a simple explanation for what was happening; Dora was probably absorbed in a computer game and had the knife to cut an apple.

Christine retrieved the phone from her work bag and walked down the hallway until she reached the office door. When she looked inside the room, lit only by the light radiating from the computer screen, she almost dropped the phone. There were two people inside. One looked like Dora, sitting at the computer, but she could not tell for sure because the hood of the sweatshirt she was wearing hid her face. But more disturbing was the tall, dark figure in the room's corner. She told herself that it was nothing more than shadows playing tricks on her eyes, making her think it was a man. The moonlight coming in through the window was forming shadows on the walls from the trees outside. But that was not what was causing what she was seeing. It was a man whose head almost reached the ceiling, and it was black—inky black. It moved like a person who was shifting his weight from one leg to the other, watching her.

Christine's throat was tight and her voice shaky. "Dora, honey, are you okay?"

The person at the computer kept staring at the monitor.

Christine brought her phone up from her side and touched the dial pad icon. That simple act caused Dora to look at her with eyes that appeared to glow yellow from the computer screen's light. She had dark circles around her eyes. It was as though she was wearing a mask, but she wasn't.

"Give me the phone, mother." Dora's voice was not her own; it was deep, like a man's. She stood up and began walking toward Christine.

That was when Christine noticed the knife in Dora's hand. "Put the knife down; we'll talk." Christine's hands quivered as she backed into the hallway. She could feel an icy coldness radiate from her daughter's body. What kind of sickness was this?

Dora swatted the phone from Christine's hand before she could complete the call to the police. Then she forced her mother against the wall with the strength of two men.

Christine felt the tip of the knife's blade press against the side of her abdomen. The shadow man was now right behind Dora and fully formed. She saw the faceless man's dark suit and the gray skin that clung to the bones of the emancipated thing. Terrified, she could barely speak. "Why are you doing this?"

"Because, mother, it is what we must do."

At that moment, she felt the sharp blade break through her skin and penetrate her organs. She screamed. But before another scream could exit her throat, the bloody steel sliced through it. Red blood was pumped through the severed artery and sprayed against the white wall.

Dora let loose of the body as it collapsed to the floor.

As the body lay on the carpet, dying, Slenderman spoke inside Dora's head. "Well done, child. Your reward is close at hand."

Chapter 6

PACIE BIT INTO A slice of her morning toast, smothered in the homemade strawberry jam and sat it back down on the paper plate next to her computer. She wiped her sticky fingers with a napkin and then clicked the button on the screen that sent the kidnapping article that she had finished writing earlier that morning to Irma who would then edit it before posting it to the website and sending it off to the local news, complete with images.

She turned on the television in her office and tuned to WBLA. The early morning news talked about a new K9, a two-year-old German shepherd named Leo, the latest member of the Black Water Police Department; and illegal salmon fishing at a dam, the next county over. Pacie knew that just because there were no other reports of abductions did not mean the guy split town.

Pacie was about to take another bite of toast when her cellphone rang. It was Irma.

"Pacie, I know it's early, but we have to go to a house." Irma seemed frantic.

"What's going on? Are you alright?"

"No, not really." Irma's voice trembled. "I had a nightmare. No, not a nightmare, a vision. I saw a woman being murdered and I think the kidnapper who took that little girl from the park yesterday had something to do with it."

Pacie did not know what to think, other than Irma certainly believed what she was saying. "It sounds more like a nightmare."

Irma huffed. "Pacie, it was real. I saw it and I also saw the house and I'm sure I'll be able to find it. We should go over there right now and call the police."

"Ah, maybe we should see if your vision is real before we call the police. But I'll be right over and pick you up."

"Hurry," Irma said, disconnecting the call.

Pacie sat there a moment, staring at the open Word document on the computer screen. What was going on? Irma saw a real-life murder in a dream? How could she know that?

"I sure hope you're wrong, Irma," Pacie said aloud as she retrieved her satchel from the bedroom. She slung it over her shoulder, rushed downstairs, and walked out the door leading to the garage, locking it behind her.

The SUV's clock read 5 a.m. as she backed out of the garage and drove onto the street. The sun would rise in an hour.

Pacie was the only car on the road that hazy Sunday morning. Past the car's headlights, a gray mist obscured buildings and street signs. She felt isolated and alone as she drove cautiously down the streets; half expecting a dog, a person, or something else to run out from the fog and into her path.

When she arrived at Irma's, she was already standing

outside waiting for her, smoking a cigarette. Pacie stopped next to her. Irma dropped her cigarette into the steel outdoor ashtray before getting inside the car with her backpack.

"Head toward Sugar Sand Park," Irma said, unzipping her fanny pack. She partially pulled out a pack of menthols, making sure she had them and then re-zipped it. "I'm gonna need these."

"I take it your no-smoking plan isn't working," Pacie said, driving out of the lot. "I thought you were going to switch to e-cigs. They have to be better than those."

"I haven't gotten around to it yet. But I'd be doing alright if it weren't for all this stressful stuff going on and the fact that I haven't had much sleep lately." Irma looked ahead. "Turn right on Walnut when you get there."

"So what exactly did you see in your—vision?"

Irma looked at Pacie. "I haven't told you yet, but I've been sleepwalking. I have a sleep study scheduled for Monday night at the hospital. Can you go with me?"

"Of course I can. How long has this been going on?"

"Not long, just the last week or so, but something is happening to me."

Pacie stopped at a flashing red light. She looked down the damp street where a light fog obscured the streetlights. The town was so empty of life it looked like a scene out of a horror movie. She drove on. "Tell me about this vision that we're going to check out."

Irma paused, then said, "I was sleeping, partially sleeping like sleep paralysis, but it wasn't. I was looking through the eyes of a young teenager. It was all fuzzy, but I saw her pick up a knife and then..."

Pacie glanced over at Irma. "And then what?"

"And then stab her mother to death." Irma looked away.

Pacie stopped the car and stared at Irma's shaking head. "Oh my god. That's horrible."

Irma looked at Pacie with wide eyes. "I also saw the man. No, not a man, the thing. The tall, dark creature that seemed to tell the girl what to do. He wore a black suit like the witnesses said and was always standing near me, I mean, near her. The girl."

Pacie pulled the car back on the road. They drove past Sugar Sand Park. It was as dismal as downtown. "I sure hope that what you saw was just a dream."

"Me too, but it was too real. I mean," Irma took a cigarette from the pack and held it in her hand. "I was there. How and why, I don't know."

"Did the entity say anything?"

Irma looked ahead at the road. "It was in the girl's head, and in my head. Its garbled voice was hard to understand, but it talked about what must be done to gain a reward."

"What had to be done, the murder? And what reward?"

"It's all fuzzy, but I think the girl was partly, more like completely, under its control. And I also remember seeing her writing in a journal."

Pacie slowed the car. "This is Walnut."

"Drive slow. I'm hoping I'll know which house it is."

Houses lined the road on both sides, most of which had darkened windows.

Irma looked left and right, then blurted out, "Stop."

Pacie stopped in the road. "Which house?"

"That one there with the lights on," Irma said, pointing to the left.

"You mean the one with the pointed arch over the front door?"

"Yes, I believe so."

"There's a car in the driveway, so someone's home."

"A dead someone."

"Can you tell if that thing or the girl is still inside?"

"No, but I get the feeling they're gone."

Pacie pulled along the side of the road. "We're going to make complete fools out of ourselves."

"I doubt it."

"At least since there are lights on, we won't be waking anyone up."

"Your right, we won't be waking anyone up." Irma put the cigarette back in her pouch.

They got out of the vehicle and stood there. It was so silent, not even a dog was barking. It was as though a slumber had befallen the neighborhood.

Pacie put her satchel on crossbody and took out a small flashlight. Irma removed the video camera from the backpack on the floor.

"People are going to think we're thieves?" Pacie said as Irma walked around the front of the car and stood next to her.

The sky above them was lightening as the sun neared the point of raising its rosy head above the horizon.

Pacie took her phone from her back pocket and zoomed in on one of the lighted windows. "The curtains are closed;

I can't see inside."

"Let's get closer," Irma said, walking across the street.

They walked up the driveway. Pacie shined her light inside the car; so far everything looked normal.

"We'll need to walk around the house," Pacie whispered. "We might be able to see in a window on the backside."

They walked through wet grass, past hip-height evergreen hedges, stopping when they saw a kitchen window with open curtains.

"I'm feeling like such a peeping Tom," Pacie said. "We'll be in such trouble if your so-called vision is wrong."

"I don't think it is," Irma said, walking up to the window. She stood on tiptoes and peered inside.

"What do you see?"

"Nothing. Just some dirty dishes."

Pacie took her turn looking in the window. There were no signs that a disturbance had occurred—like a murder. She listened. No sounds were coming from inside.

They stumbled over a garden hose as they walked through the shadows next to the house. When they rounded the corner, they saw a backdoor that opened onto a deck. The deck light was off, leaving distant streetlamps to light the backyard. A strong breeze caused shadows, cast by tree limbs, to dance like rubbery silhouettes of people, unable to move past the picket fence.

Pacie had no problem letting Irma take the lead. She followed her up the deck steps to the backdoor. When Irma yelped and held her hands over her mouth, Pacie knew she had seen something that scared her. She rushed up and looked in the backdoor window. The dimly lit hallway had an object lying on the floor next to a room that cast a flickering light out its door.

"That's a body," Pacie said, not believing what she was looking at.

Irma turned on her video camera, opened the backdoor, and walked inside.

"You didn't put your gloves on," Pacie said, donning a pair of disposable gloves she kept in her satchel.

"Oh, yeah, I forgot." Irma took a pair from her fanny pack.

"We should call the police before we contaminate things."

"Wait. I need to see," Irma said, wiping the doorknob as she entered the home.

"See what?" Pacie said, rushing up to the bloody body. She knelt and felt for a pulse in the wrist, avoiding the cut neck. "She's not breathing and there's no pulse. She's dead." Pacie stood up. "I smell that same stench from the trail."

"I knew it."

Pacie watched Irma walk into the office. "What are you doing?"

Still recording, Irma walked around the desk so she could see what was playing on the computer. Her hand shook as she lowered the camera and pointed toward the monitor. "I, I..."

Pacie walked next to Irma. Freaky images flashed onto the screen every few seconds; images that portrayed death in its various forms. The oddest thing was that they looked like real pictures of real events that someone had taken while watching a person perform the deviant act. A young boy next to a kiddie pool holding a kitten under the water. Feminine hands strangling a woman in bed. And most disturbing, an image of the woman in the hallway being stabbed. "What the hell sick kind of shit is this?"

"I saw this?" Irma looked away from the computer.

Pacie took a picture of the URL on the screen. "In your vision?"

Irma looked reluctantly at Pacie. "It was one of my sleep-walking events. I woke up to find myself looking at these images on my computer. I didn't remember going to my desk, let alone going to this website."

"Did you see these exact images?"

"Similar images with strange symbols and things."

"I'm calling the police," Pacie said.

"Not yet," Irma said. "There's still the journal I saw in the vision. It's probably upstairs in the girl's bedroom."

The pair walked out of the office, stepping hesitantly over the body. They moved like stealthy cats as they walked past the kitchen and living room to the staircase. They nodded at each other, then climbed the steps to the second floor. One room had a light on.

Pacie grabbed Irma's arm, stopping her from moving any farther, and mouthed to her that the killer could be in there. Then her jaw dropped when she thought of the dead woman downstairs. Pacie whispered, "I don't remember seeing the knife that you said was used to kill the poor woman. So where is it?"

They both looked at the room. Pacie took a jackknife from her satchel and unfolded the blade. They crept, inch by inch, toward the room, listening for the slightest of sounds.

Irma reached the doorway first. She poked her camera slowly around the doorjamb and looked inside through the viewfinder, but she could not angle it enough to see much. Then she walked through the door and into the room.

Pacie pulled the ill-fitting gloves tighter on her hands and continued gripping the blade handle.

"No one's in here," Irma said, walking to the bed where a book lay on the covers.

Pacie knelt and shined her light under the bed; board games and a teddy bear were all she saw. Then she stood and looked at the closed closet door.

"This is the journal," Irma said, recording its pages as she flipped them one by one.

Pacie did not want to open the closet door. If someone was hiding in there, that's where she wanted them to stay. "Hurry up."

"Look at this," Irma said, holding the journal so that Pacie could see the page with a hand-drawn figure of a tall, skinny man wearing a black suit. "She drew the kidnapper."

Pacie agreed; it looked just like the witnesses' descriptions, and this teen, whoever she was, gave it a name—Slenderman.

"Slenderman. I think there is an actual creature called Slenderman," Irma said, closing the journal, leaving it as she had found it. "Now it's time to call the police and get out of here."

"I'll call as soon as we get back in the car, just in case the cops get here before we're out of the house."

They walked down the staircase and to the hallway. The body lay as it had been. They stepped over it and walked back out the door they had come in.

The morning sky had brightened, yet the fog still hung over the neighborhood. They walked at a pace that would not draw attention as they made their way back to the car. They took off their gloves before getting inside and placed them in a plastic grocery bag that Pacie used to collect trash.

"I'm ready to call," Pacie said. "We didn't leave anything inside, did we?"

"No, everything should be just as we found it. Except for the doorknob that I wiped," Irma said, taking the cigarette from her pouch. She cracked her window. "Do you mind?"

Pacie shook her head and called 9-1-1, giving only the information needed to send the police to the house to investigate the murder.

"Are we waiting here?" Irma asked.

"Yeah, I want to talk to Haley, if she's one of the people that respond."

Within minutes, they heard sirens approaching.

"I'm glad they know your car," Irma said. "That way we don't look like suspects lurking around the murder scene."

"Right, they probably think we're here because you heard the call on your scanner."

"Which could so totally be true."

Pacie looked down at her phone and searched the term Slenderman while Irma looked at the recording on her camera's viewfinder.

"According to this," Pacie began, "Slenderman is a fictional supernatural character that originated as a creepypasta meme. He's described as a thin, unnaturally tall humanoid with a featureless head and face, wearing a black suit. He's known to stalk, traumatize, and abduct people, particularly children. Oh, and this is weird; sometimes he has tentacles."

"Yeah, totally freaky. But," Irma said, tapping cigarette ashes out the window, "I think there are some authentic murder cases based on Slenderman. I'll have to do some research on it."

Now surrounded by police cars and officers, they could not leave if they had wanted to.

"There's Haley," Pacie said, waving at her as she walked toward the house. "I don't think she saw me."

"Look at that guy," Irma said, pointing toward a man who was standing on the sidewalk, several houses down.

"Who?"

"That guy way down there. He's extremely tall and is wearing black."

Pacie saw the man watching the commotion. "Are you thinking he could be the killer?"

"We should talk to him," Irma said, opening the car door. "I'll keep my camera facing away, or toward the ground so that he won't know that I'm recording him. Can't have too much research material, ya know."

"I'm coming with you."

They got out of the car and walked down the sidewalk toward the lanky young man.

The man seemed to ignore them as they approached, but he did not walk away.

Pacie cleared her throat as she and Irma stopped near him. "We don't get much excitement around here. Do you know what's going on back there?"

The twenty-something wore sunglasses even though the fog had not completely lifted. "Nope."

"I don't think I've seen you around here before," Pacie said, fishing for information. "Are you new to the neighborhood?"

He shrugged.

Pacie could tell he did not want to talk with them. "Well, have a good day."

He nodded and walked down the sidewalk toward the crime scene.

Irma leaned toward Pacie and whispered, "He's acting a little suspicious."

"Yeah, maybe."

They stood in place, watching him. Irma raised her camera and recorded him as he walked away. "He's over six feet tall."

"That's not nine or ten feet, plus he's not wearing a suit. And he has a face." Pacie grinned.

"His clothes are black. The kids gave a poor description."

"I don't know," Pacie said.

"Killers do hang around where they committed the crime."

"I thought you were all convinced that the kidnapper was a Bigfoot."

"Don't make fun of me," Irma said, lowering the camera. "I'm just looking at all the angles."

Pacie laughed. "I know, I'm just giving you a hard time."

"He's walking past the crime scene."

"Let's go back to the car."

"I've only scanned the girl's journal," Irma said, walking next to Pacie, "but it appears she was obsessed with Slenderman and that demons were tormenting her."

"I wonder if a satanic cult found its way to Black Water."

"It's a possibility."

"Look, Haley's coming back out of the house," Pacie said. "Let's see if she'll talk with us."

Detective Wanat saw them as she walked toward her car. "May I ask you ladies, how you knew about the murder? I have a hunch that it was you two that called it in."

"I saw it in a dream," Irma said, walking up to the detective.

"Really?" Det. Wanat said as she opened her car door.

"It was like a vision—so real. I called Pacie, and we went looking for the house I saw in the dream."

"If I didn't know you two, I'd be taking you downtown for questioning because you seem to know too much."

"Glad you know us." Pacie smiled.

"Did you both go inside the house?" Det. Wanat waited for their answer.

"Ah." Pacie was not sure how to answer the question without lying.

"I saw the whole thing in my dream," Irma said again. "But we might have looked in a window ... or something."

"I knew it."

"Is there anything you can tell us?" Pacie asked.

"Not currently, other than it is a murder scene. Besides, I think you guys know as much as I do right now."

"Is the body the only person in the home?" Pacie asked.

"Yes." Det. Wanat said.

"Did you find the knife?" Irma asked.

"You two look guilty as hell," Det. Wanat said.

"I saw it in my vision," Irma said.

Detective Wanat shook her head. "Not yet."

"I know who killed her?" Irma blurted out.

Detective Wanat's eyes widened. "Who?"

"The daughter."

"How do you know this?"

"My vision, of course."

"Of course."

"Do you think the murder has anything to do with the kidnapping at Sugar Sand Park?" Pacie asked.

"I don't have enough information yet," Det. Wanat said. "It's possible, but I'm not seeing a connection."

"I see a connection," Irma said. "The daughter's journal—"

Detective Wanat interrupted, "The journal? How did you see the journal?"

Irma did not answer as she looked over at Pacie.

"Irma has a sleep study on Monday because of her nightmares," Pacie said, deflecting an answer with a truth.

"You two know I love you both and I want to help you out because the community adores and trusts you, the same as I do," Det. Wanat said as she looked down at their feet. "My gut tells me you both have been inside the house. I'll help you out, just don't disturb the crime scenes."

Pacie looked down at the wet grass clippings stuck to their shoes and then back up at Det. Wanat, who was staring back at her.

Neither Pacie nor Irma admitted to going inside. Instead, they stood there as if they had not heard the comment.

"You both be careful," Det. Wanat said. She reached inside the car and took out a box of disposable gloves. "If it is the same guy, he just might come for you two next."

Chapter 7

"NOW WHAT?" IRMA SAID as they walked back to the SUV.

"Let's go back to your place and go through what we have so far. Especially that weird website."

The fog still hung in the air when they arrived at Irma's.

The minute they walked into Irma's apartment, the Staffie was prancing about, making it known that he needed to go outside.

"I need to take Mr. Dibble for a walk. I'll be right back," Irma said, placing her backpack on the dining table.

"I'll get a pot of coffee started," Pacie said, walking into the kitchen.

"I don't know if I need caffeine," Irma said with the leash in hand. "My adrenaline is still pumping from that ... murder."

"Mine, too. Just a habit, I guess," Pacie said, taking the coffee from the cupboard.

While the coffee brewed, Pacie walked to the front window and raised the blinds. She looked out on downtown Black Water. Through the thinning fog, she watched the traffic light change from red to green. One lone car drove slowly down the street.

She turned and looked at the apartment. Dirty dishes were not only scattered on the kitchen counters but also the coffee table and desk. A rumpled blanket lay on the couch and the kitchen trash can was overflowing. Something must be wrong because Irma rarely kept her home this messy.

The coffee pot clicked. Pacie took the last clean mug from the cupboard, poured herself half a cup, and sat at the computer.

Pacie typed in the PIN to move past the screensaver and unlocked the laptop. She looked at her phone and pulled up the picture of the computer screen at the murder house and was about to type in the URL when Irma opened the apartment door.

"That was fast," Pacie said, looking back at Irma and Mr. Dibble.

"All we did was take care of business."

Mr. Dibble ran to Pacie. She leaned over and petted the pooch on the head. "How are you today, Mr. Dibble?"

The Staffie danced a moment before racing to his food dish where Irma was filling with dry kibble.

"You have such a cheerful dog," Pacie said.

"I wish I was as happy as him," Irma said, walking over to Pacie. "Have you looked up anything?"

Pacie turned back to the computer. "I was getting ready to put in the address of the web page we saw on that house's computer."

Irma's body tensed.

"Are you alright?"

Irma held onto the edge of the desk. "I don't know."

Pacie stood up. "Sit down. I'll get another chair."

Irma sat at the computer while Pacie placed a dining chair next to Irma.

"Have you been sleeping?"

"No, not really."

"What time do you want me to pick you up tomorrow for your sleep study?"

Irma thought a moment. "Doctor Plum said to be there around nine, so I guess get here around eight-thirty."

"Do you want to spend the night at my house tonight?"

Irma shrugged. "I'll be fine here, it's just one more night."

"Well, think about it."

"If something's going to happen, it will happen there just as well as it can here."

"You're right, but at least I'll be around," Pacie said. "And I'm a light sleeper. If you happen to sleepwalk, I'll probably hear you."

Pacie held up her phone so that Irma could see the web address. "Type this in."

Irma began typing in the URL but stopped.

"What's wrong?"

Irma took her hands off the keyboard. "I don't know if it's a good idea. There might be a subliminal message that could come through."

"I suppose. But I don't think subliminal messages work all that well."

"I remember reading that back in the late nineteen-fif-ties, movie theaters wanted to make more money so they would flash split-second messages like drink Coca-Cola or eat popcorn. Only the subconscious mind could see them," Irma said. "And it worked."

"On a single frame?"

"It would have to be."

"Would you be able to find subliminal messages on the website?"

"Only if I could download the video and play it in my software."

"We should at least check it out because it was on that computer where the girl killed her mom, or at least I suppose it was a mother and daughter. If she had the website address, her friends probably have it too. I don't want other kids being affected by it and another person being murdered."

"Okay, let's do it." Irma finished typing in the web address and pressed enter. The screen went black.

"What happened? Did your computer just die?"

Irma moved the mouse around and fiddled with the power cable. She was about to restart the laptop when the screen flashed on with a momentary blast of bright white light, then a disturbing slideshow began playing. Not images of cuddly kittens or cute little puppies, but images of death. A dead raven, a corpse in a morgue, and a snake eating a mouse. Even the symbols that randomly took screen time were disturbing. Some strokes looked like the texture of a rat's tail, while others were slivers of torn skin and muscle.

"Why would anyone watch this sickening thing?"

"I watched it, but not by choice," Irma said. "Thankfully I don't much remember it."

"Can you tell if you can download a video of it?"

Irma clicked around. "I think so."

"You're not working on it here by yourself. Come back to the house with me. I won't accept no for an answer."

"Do you think we're being exposed to subliminal messages right now?"

Pacie looked at the images cycling every few seconds. "I have no doubt, but I'll bet they only affect the impressionable. At least I hope so. If not, we're doomed."

"You had to say that didn't you?" Irma closed the browser tab. "I don't want to look at it anymore. Everyone, even us, are impressionable to some degree."

"I'm thinking of calling the police," Pacie said, "but they must know about this site because it was on the computer at that house this morning and I'm sure they've found and read the journal, so they know about all of this."

Irma connected her video camera to the computer. "Let's look at the video I took of the journal."

"Good idea."

"Here we go. I'll pause it page to page."

The first several pages read like a normal diary. The young girl talked of school, the new neighborhood boy, and everyday events.

"There's nothing unusual in this part," Pacie said.

With each turn of the page after that, the entries grew darker. Hand scribbled images of a faceless man began filling the pages along with words about him wanting her to do something to get a reward.

"Go back," Pacie said. "What was the date when things

changed?"

Irma rewound the recording. "Looks like the first of June. Just a couple of weeks ago."

"Did anything happen in Black Water at that time?"

"Like what?"

"I don't know. Anything new or out of the ordinary."

"I can't think of anything."

"Me either. We'll have to go through the newspaper."

Irma continued going through the video.

"She first mentioned Slenderman a week ago," Irma said. "And something about going to live at a palace."

"Stop there," Pacie said, scooting her chair closer to the monitor. "Her handwriting has gone from normal to broken words."

"It's like something has taken her over."

"What does that say?" Pacie pointed to a sentence.

"It's something about her and her friends creating something. I think it says, we did it. We created a tulpa, here in my room. But it looked different from what we imagined, and then he faded away."

"What's on the next page?"

Irma moved through the frames, stopping on the next page. She zoomed in. "He came again tonight, a tall man dressed in black. This time was easier, but it was still not the pony. Instead, we got this thing. We created this thing who calls himself Slenderman. His form was more filled out and he growled. We screamed and ran out of the house. Now I'm really afraid, but I had to come back to my bedroom before mom got home from work. My friends refused to come with me and instead went home. I don't see him right now."

"They created or summoned something. A spirit or demon."

"Slenderman," Irma said with trepidation.

"It's like tulpamancy. Where people use some type of occult practice where they use thoughts and emotions to bring about, so-called, real things."

"How and why?"

"I know little about it, but I think they use meditation or lucid dreaming, stuff like that. I only know about it because I remember hearing about people creating tulpas from their favorite characters like My Little Pony. They believe they created real living beings. The Internet makes it easy for young people to find out about this stuff and get drawn in."

"So it sounds like some innocent young teens, trying to create a pony, ended up bringing Slenderman to Black Water instead."

"I think you're right. You and Mr. Dibble are definitely coming to my house. Pack up your laptop and whatever else you need," Pacie said. "The bedroom down the hallway from mine has a desk. It's clean, and I aired it out last week. You can set up there, for now."

"I guess it's a good idea," Irma said, closing the laptop. "Come on, Mr. Dibble, we're spending the night at Pacie's."

Chapter 8

BEN POUNDED HIS HEAD on the bathroom wall in his beachside Black Water home, leaving a rounded indentation in the white drywall.

Life was good, living with his girlfriend Anna in her parents' rental. That is, until Anna showed him the website. Not only did thoughts of obediently serving this thing who called himself Slenderman, but urges to obey his commands became acceptable. Even Anna began inviting friends over and showing them the video.

Ben splashed water on his face. When he wiped it dry, he noticed his skin looked dull and sickly. He needed more sun.

He walked down the hallway to the bedroom where Anna was still in bed with the laptop resting on her legs, appearing to be almost in a trance.

"We have to stop watching that," Ben said, sitting next to her on the bed. "There's something about it and I just don't feel right."

Anna continued to stare at the gruesome slideshow. "I can't. It's talking to me. Doesn't it talk to you?"

Ben put his hand on her arm. "It's driving me insane, and I think it's doing the same to you. When you invited people over to perform tulpamancy with you, I think you crossed the line."

Anna looked at Ben. "But don't you feel it?"

"I feel like we've gotten ourselves into something we can't get out of."

Anna leaned into Ben. "I don't want to get out of it. Slenderman will give us our reward when we present the kids to him. And today is the day. They'll be here soon for bible study."

"This is so effed up. Their parents think they're going to be studying about Jesus and here we are, good church-going people, giving them to this entity we summoned who is likely going to take them to Hell."

Anna gripped his arm so tight that he winced. "If it's not them, then it's us. He'll take us to Hell if we don't do what he says. No one will notice. When we summon him, we'll present our gifts, and both of us and Slenderman will be happy. We'll get riches and have a comfortable life. Neither of us will ever have to work again, and we will be joyful. You know my parents said they are going to kick us out if we don't catch up on the rent. Besides, I'm compelled to do this. And so are you."

Ben gently pulled Anna's face to his. "You're right. I am too, it makes me excited."

She kissed his lips. "Slenderman has given us a gift. A promise that everything we do will be better and more enjoyable. Even allowing us to visit his palace."

Between kisses, Ben said, "I worry about going to jail, though. I don't think we can pull this off."

"We can pull this off. Slenderman said his presence will mesmerize the town and everyone will obey his every word. And since we are among the first to help him, he will help us. We'll blame it on that new guy in town."

Crawling under the covers next to Anna's warm body, Ben said, "To think I almost backed out. I trust Slenderman, he's my Jesus."

Chapter 9

"IT SMELLS LIKE STRAWBERRIES in here," Irma said as she walked in the front door of Pacie's mansion.

"Follow me," Pacie said.

Irma sat her suitcase and backpack by the staircase and followed Pacie through the dining room and study, finally reaching the kitchen. She saw several jars of jam lined up neatly on the counter next to a well-preserved fireplace.

"Don't forget to take your jam with you when you leave," Pacie said, sliding a few jars off to the side.

"Don't worry, I won't forget," Irma said, walking back out to the central passage.

Pacie picked up the suitcase and began walking up the steps. "Follow me. I'll put you in the blue room."

Irma grabbed her backpack and held tight to the handrail as she followed Pacie up the grand staircase. "I'm surprised you didn't call it a bedchamber."

Pacie laughed. "I don't know why you and Mr. Dibble don't live here with me. You know I have the room."

Irma followed Pacie through the first door on the left.

"I like my privacy. Besides, if I have to get up in the middle of the night and use the bathroom—I have to walk a mile just to get to it."

"Use the one in my bedroom. Just walk across the hallway and through the green room. You can use mine. I won't lock the doors."

"I guess I'll have to."

"Do you want to use the bedchamber downstairs, instead?" Pacie smiled.

"No, this is fine. People walking into the house will be able to see into my room."

"I don't get many visiters." Pacie sat the suitcase on the white, floral embroidered bedspread of the canopy bed. "You should be comfortable in here. Are you hungry?"

Irma sat her backpack on the desk and took out her laptop. "Yes and no. I'm hungry, but I have knots in my stomach. I think I'll take a catnap. Whatever is going on with me is zapping all my energy."

"I noticed. You're not your usual peppy self," Pacie said, grinning. She slid up the window sash. "There's sliced ham in the fridge and other stuff you can eat when you're hungry. If you can't find me when you wake up, I'll likely be outside somewhere or in my office writing."

Irma opened the suitcase and took out a blouse. She gave it a shake as she walked to the closet. "I'll put away my things and then lay down."

Pacie went downstairs and into the study. She sat down at her computer, pushing aside the cold soggy toast from earlier, and opened the latest mystery novel she was writing.

She wanted to look out a window to see if the fog was thinning, but when they added the addition onto the mansion, the windows needed to be sacrificed. One was now a door to the kitchen, the other the door to the bathroom. She lightly drummed her fingertips on the laptop's keyboard. "I can't think."

After completing two pages, rough pages, Pacie looked at the clock. It was noon and her stomach was growling. She was about to take the plate into the kitchen when she heard a scream. It was Irma. Pacie ran up the steps and into Irma's room.

Irma was standing beside her bed, putting on her fanny pack. "We have to go. We have to go now."

"What do you mean? Go where?" Pacie watched Irma sling her backpack over a shoulder. "Did you have another vision?"

"I did, and we have to go so that we can save the kids." Irma rushed past Pacie and down the staircase, with Mr. Dibble close behind her.

"Wait a minute," Pacie said, following her. "What did you see?"

Irma stopped at the front door and turned around. "I saw a half-dozen young kids about to be given to Slenderman. It hasn't happened yet, but it will at any moment. That's why we have to go now."

Pacie grabbed her satchel and followed Irma and Mr. Dibble out the door to the car parked in the driveway. "I take it you know where all this is happening?"

"Just like before," Irma said. "I'll know it when I see it."

"Where are we heading? Walnut again?"

"No, it's one of the beach houses," Irma said, fumbling with a cigarette. "It's near North Beach."

Pacie drove onto the street, watching Irma's hands shake like a person with Parkinson's disease. "Are you alright?"

"No, of course not," Irma snapped. "I'm sorry, I don't mean to be so short with you but there's no time to waste."

Pacie nodded. "I know."

When they reached North Beach, Pacie said, "Which way?"

Irma looked left and right and appeared to be holding back tears. "Go right and drive slow."

Pacie turned right and slowly drove down the street; the beach was on the left and cottages were on the right. "I can't believe it's still foggy outside. I think the fog is thicker here. This is really weird weather."

"Pull over here," Irma said. She pointed to an upmarket two-story house. "I think it's that one."

Pacie parked in a horizontal spot, turned off the SUV, and looked at the charming white house sitting on a small embankment. "How are we going to do this?"

"Let's just go up to the door and knock. We'll say we're neighbors or something and ... I don't know," Irma said, getting out of the car. She dropped her cigarette onto the sidewalk and snuffed it out with the sole of her shoe. Mr. Dibble watched her through the window. "I'll be right back, Mr. Dibble."

Pacie held her phone in her hand as she followed Irma up the wooden steps to the landing. The clomp of their steps as they climbed, and the sweet fragrance of peonies seemed somehow off—the sound dull and the scent sour. Even the tubes and sail of the wind chime hanging from the home's awning did not move, making not a single clang. Combined with the lingering fog, they added to the eerie feeling.

The curtains were closed; Irma could not see inside. She rang the doorbell. Moments later, a young woman opened the door.

"Hi," the pretty young woman said. "Are you the new family?"

When Irma did not answer right away, Pacie worried whether they were going to pull this off.

The young woman looked at Irma and then at Pacie. "My name's Anna. Where's your daughter?"

Pacie stepped closer to Irma so she could see past Anna's body. Children sat in a circle on the floor. "She's in the car. We just wanted to be sure we were at the right place."

"You are," Anna said, holding the door only partway open. "We were just about to get started."

"Can we come in?" Irma said.

"We have quiet time before bible study, it's like meditation so we try not to disturb the children. It brings them closer to Christ."

Pacie saw a young man, deliberately staying out of view, hand Anna a clipboard and pen.

"Thanks, Ben." Anna held it out for Irma to take. "I just need a signature. It makes it all legal. Don't want anyone thinking any shenanigans are going on."

Irma took the clipboard and looked down at the papers. "I'd like to go inside before I sign this. I'm sure you understand."

Pacie could tell the girl was getting annoyed by the way

she pulled the door closer to herself, making it near impossible to see inside any more than she already had. Pacie did not know what to do. They had no daughter in the car, and the glimpses she saw inside did not show that the kids were in any distress. They had two options, one was to walk away, and the other was to force themselves inside. But then what? If Irma's vision was wrong, or they had the wrong house, and they forced themselves inside, the homeowners would certainly call the police on them. Pacie wished she could read Irma's mind. "Maybe we should leave."

Irma handed the clipboard back to Anna. "I'm sorry."

"Me too." Anna took the clipboard and abruptly closed the door.

Pacie and Irma walked back down the steps and got in the SUV.

"Well, there were kids inside, but they didn't look like they were in danger," Pacie said, starting the car. "Are you sure this is the right place?"

"I'm sure," Irma said. "I saw the wind chime. Park around the corner where they can't see us."

Pacie drove to the other side of the block and parked. "What should we do now? If we call the police and nothing bad is going on when they get here, the police will think we're nuts and not listen to us anymore, especially when you tell them it's based on a vision you had."

Irma sighed. "I know. But I'm sure I'm right."

"One hundred percent?"

"Ninety-nine percent." Irma lit another cigarette. "We need evidence before that man takes the kids."

"Slenderman?"

"I know it sounds crazy."

"Let's get the evidence we need then," Pacie said. "The only problem is that it's broad daylight and people will see us snooping around."

"It's still pretty foggy," Irma said. "Maybe we can get close enough to see inside."

"The windows I saw had their curtains closed," Pacie said.

"Or maybe," Irma said, reaching inside her pack again. She held up a wallet with a police badge and identification card inside. "We could use this."

Pacie looked at the card, squinting to read the name on it. "Well, Detective Carol Thomas, what are we going to do with the kids when we get them out of the house—if they let us take them, which I doubt."

"Other than watching the house for suspicious activity, I don't know what else to do."

"Well, we could at least do that until we figure something else out," Pacie said, checking to make sure she still had her small, folding binoculars inside her satchel. "Ready to walk to the beach across from the house?"

Irma looked at her watch. "It's noon. I can't imagine a bible study for young children to last more than an hour or so."

"Let's do it," Pacie said, watching Irma let Mr. Dibble out of the car.

They walked down the sidewalk toward the beach. An eerie calm accompanied the wispy fog. It was midday and the mist covering Black Water should have burned off as daylight dawned, but it still hung over the roads and hugged the buildings.

"Later, when I have time," Pacie said as they crossed the road to a small playground with swings, slides, and monkey bars, "I'm going to check the weather forecast and find out what's up with this fog."

Irma looked out over the still water of the Great Lake. "Even the waves are barely moving. This is not helping my nerves."

"Let's set down." Pacie ran a finger on the seat of a bench. "It's wet. Do you have something to wipe this off inside that backpack of yours?"

Irma brought out a pack of tissue. She wiped a couple of spots and put the sopping wet tissues in a trash can. "I think we're still going to get wet."

They sat down, slightly off-angle from the house so that they did not look like they were staring directly at it.

Pacie brought her small pair of binoculars to her eyes and looked at the house. "The curtains are still closed, and I don't see anything abnormal."

"Let me see." Irma took the binoculars that Pacie handed her. "I wish these could see through walls or at least have some type of infrared heat detection."

"I'm not that high-tech." Pacie laughed.

Irma handed the binoculars back to Pacie. "When the parents come to pick up their kids, we'll know more."

"Right, everything will either be completely normal and your vision was wrong, or—"

"My vision is right," Irma interrupted.

"Or your vision is working to save lives."

Pacie and Irma sat on the bench for nearly an hour before walking to the gently lapping water. Mr. Dibble waded into the freshwater lake and quenched his thirst.

The coarse caw of a raven caught Pacie's attention. She looked around, attempting to locate the bird through the never-ending fog. When it cawed again, she saw it perched on the chimney of the house they were staking out. A moment of fear crept inside Pacie because it was as though the raven was warning of an approaching threat—possibly from the so-called Slenderman.

"A car's pulling up," Irma said. "If it's one of the parents, we'll know momentarily if something happened to the kids."

Pacie looked through her binoculars and watched a woman get out of the car and walk up the steps. She knocked on the door. Anna answered it and soon a young girl walked out. "Looks like things are fine."

"Let me see," Irma said, reaching for the binoculars.

"Maybe it's the wrong day," Pacie said.

"I suppose." Irma handed the binoculars back to Pacie. "Let's get closer."

They walked toward the road as other cars approached. Kids were reunited with their parents. None had come up missing.

Irma turned to Pacie. "I guess it was a false alarm. But it seemed so real."

"We can come back next Sunday."

Irma shrugged. "I guess we can leave."

They crossed to the sidewalk on the other side of the road. Irma pulled on Pacie's arm. "Another car just pulled up.

Let's watch."

They stopped and watched a woman walk up the steps to the door. The woman kept knocking when no one answered.

"Let's walk back that way," Pacie said.

The woman was now banging on the door.

"Something's wrong," Irma said, picking up her pace.

They stopped at the foot of the stairs leading up to Anna's front door.

"Is something wrong?" Pacie shouted up to the frantic woman who was now trying to open the door but was unable.

The woman turned and looked wide-eyed at Mr. Dibble, and then at them as they rushed up the steps. Her voice quivered. "My son Seth is in there, and no one is answering the door or the phone."

"What does Seth look like?"

The woman could barely speak. "He has on a blue T-shirt and jeans. He's only ten years old. Please help."

"Call the police," Pacie said to the woman gripping her cellphone.

Irma clung to a handrail as if she were about to collapse. "It's coming true."

Pacie tried the door, but it would not budge. Curtains covered the windows, making it impossible to see inside.

"The police are on their way," the woman said.

"You stay here and meet them," Pacie said to the woman. "We're going around the house." Then she turned to Irma. "I'll go left. You and Mr. Dibble go right. Can you do that?"

Irma nodded, holding Mr. Dibble's leash tight. "Let's do it."

Pacie stepped off the landing and into a flower bed of wilting peonies. Something was off. Then Pacie realized the aromatic pink flowers and all the flowers in the bed did not fill the air with their beautiful perfumes. Even the sour scent she encountered at the bottom of the steps had disappeared. The fog was still heavy, even though it was one o'clock in the afternoon. Her shoes were getting wet as she moved through the damp grass. It looked like a layer of ice crystals covered it.

Pacie tried to peer into every window that she passed. But they were either covered with heavy drapes or drawn blinds. When she reached the corner of the house, she stood still, listening for people running. Everything was muted. Not only was sound muffled, but her vision seemed to blur. She caught no hint of Irma or anyone else.

When Pacie went around the corner of the house, she jumped when she saw a human form hiding in the mist covering the backyard. She sighed with relief when she realized it was a water fountain statue of a graceful ivory female pouring water from a bucket onto lilies and into a clamshell. But there was something dark sitting on its head—a raven. It perched and sat and nothing more. Pacie half expected the raven to mutter: Nevermore, this grim, ungainly, ghastly, gaunt and ominous bird of yore.

Trying to ignore the bird that seemed to watch her, she walked along the back of the house to the patio where the back door was wide open. Had the kidnappers escaped through the back door and had Irma gone inside the house?

"Irma," Pacie said in a loud whisper. "Where are you?"

Even her own voice was suppressed. She could scream and

it would likely sound like she had a thick mask over her mouth.

Pacie stepped onto the deck just as Irma stepped onto the other side of it. She gasped. "Oh, you scared me. I didn't know you were there."

"I'm sorry, I didn't mean to scare you," Irma said, looking at the open door. "It's freaking weird back here."

"No doubt," Pacie said, standing to the side of the door. "Seth, are you in there?"

There was no answer.

Still recording with her video camera, Irma said, "I don't think anyone's in there. I think they ran out the back door."

"Let's go inside," Pacie said. "But be careful because they might have a gun and shoot at us if they're still here."

"I don't think they are," Irma said.

Pacie walked through the back door and into a laundry room. Instead of the smell of detergent and soap, there was a foul odor. "That's the same smell from the trail and that poor woman's house."

"Go to the living room where the kids were sitting in a circle," Irma said, following behind her with Mr. Dibble at her side.

Pacie walked through the kitchen and into the living room. "It feels like we're in some kind of alternate reality."

"Look at the floor," Irma said, pointing her camera at a circle of symbols. "They're the same ones from the video and that girl's journal."

"I think they had the kids sitting on these, one for each child." Pacie knelt to get a closer look at the marks in the dimness while Mr. Dibble sniffed around. "Why was only one taken?"

Pacie and Irma jumped when there was a banging at the front door.

"Police, open up."

Pacie opened the door and stepped back.

"Pacie, Irma," Officer Kline said, lowering his weapon. "What are you two doing in here?"

"We're helping that woman find her son, Seth," Pacie said, still holding up her arms. "The back door was already open, so we came inside."

"You both can lower your arms and please step outside," Officer Kline said. "Did you find anything?"

"Other than those symbols on the floor, no," Pacie said. "But I did see the kids sitting on them earlier."

"And how did you see that?" Det. Wanat said, walking inside.

"Hi, Detective," Pacie said. "Ah, we—"

"I had another vision," Irma interrupted. "I saw this house and children being taken."

"Taken by whom?" Det. Wanat said.

Irma looked down at the symbols and then back up at Haley. "By a young couple and that creepy guy that took Morgan."

"All we saw was the young woman named Anna," Pacie said. "I did catch a glimpse of a young guy that was with her. She called him Ben."

Detective Wanat looked confused.

"The truth is," Pacie said, "when Irma told me about the vision we came right over here and went to the door. That's how we know the woman and guy's name and saw the kids sitting right there. And later, when we heard a woman scream-ing, we ran back here, and she told us her son was missing so we went looking for him while she called you guys. That's all there is to it."

"The back door was open," Irma said. "They must have left through there, but I didn't hear or see anyone."

Detective Wanat nodded. "Okay, but I need you two to step outside."

Officer Kline shook as if he was shaking something off. "It's weird in here. I'm inclined to step outside with the ladies."

"You're right," Det. Wanat said. "I don't know what's going on around here, but it's not normal."

Chapter 10

"HI, PACIE — IRMA," OFFICER BLANCHARD said, breathing hard as he rushed past them, up the steps to Anna and Ben's, causing the planks beneath their feet to vibrate.

"Hi," Pacie replied, but she doubted he heard her as he dashed around the side of the house.

"Let's go back over to the park and get a video," Irma said.

Police cars packed the street as they made their way to the sidewalk on the other side.

Irma handed Pacie a cordless microphone and held up her camera. "Face me so that I can get the house in the background."

Pacie looked out over the hazy sea of water before her. The life was being drained from Black Water, leaving it weak and vulnerable. Behind her, sirens screamed, and police radios squawked.

"You can go ahead," Irma said, pointing the camera at her. "I'm recording live to all the usual places."

Pacie cleared her throat. "Hi, I'm Pacie Rose, citizen reporter, here at North Beach in Black Water, where another child has been abducted. Seth was attending a bible study at the house behind me. When his mother returned to pick him up, he was missing; along with Anna and any other bible study workers, leaving an empty house. Parents who arrived earlier could retrieve their children, but little Seth is currently missing.

Seth is ten years old and was last seen wearing a blue T-shirt and jeans. He was in a bible study with a woman in her twenties named Anna, and a young man named Ben. She has blonde hair and light-colored clothing. The male may also be traveling with them.

If you have information on Seth, or Morgan the first missing child, contact the Black Water Police Department at 555-6401.

This is Pacie Rose, citizen reporter."

Irma lowered the camera. "That should do it."

Pacie handed the microphone to Irma and looked back at the house. "The place is crawling with cops. I don't think we're needed here anymore."

"Well, what now?" Irma said, slinging the backpack over a shoulder.

"We could go to Sugar Sand Park."

Irma moaned. "And do what? Walk back down that trail?"

"Just thinking," Pacie said, shrugging. "But whatever happened here occurred from the back of the house because there wasn't anything suspicious happening in the front while we were here. Let's drive around the block and see if we find anything that looks out of the ordinary."

"I like that idea better."

They walked to the SUV. Irma put Mr. Dibble in the backseat. Then when they were all inside Pacie locked the doors.

"I'm feeling super anxious," Irma said, pushing her back-pack to the side of the foot compartment.

"Me, too," Pacie said, pulling onto the hazy side street. She drove at a slow walking pace around the block. "It's as though the fog has an ... off-sync electrical charge to it."

"Something like that," Irma said. "Stop here. I think we're directly behind the house."

With no cars behind her, or driving toward her for that matter, she stopped in her lane. "You're right."

They rolled down their windows so that they could listen to a couple of officers standing in the backyard with a track-ing dog.

"I can't hear them," Irma said, getting out of the car. "The fog is absorbing sound waves."

"I'm not surprised." As soon as Irma cleared the car, Pacie parked along the side of the road. She got out and stood next to Irma on the sidewalk.

They listened as the officers and K9 walked closer to them.

"Leo's lost the scent," the handler said, his voice sounded distant. "It's like they just ... disappeared."

Pacie waved when she noticed one of the officers looking at them. "Let's walk up to them. I think it's Frenchie."

Irma looked at Mr. Dibble, who was watching them through the car window. "I'll be right back, Mr. Dibble."

"Oh, Pacie. What's up?" Officer French said, holding the dog's leash.

"Hi, Frenchie, I thought that was you," Pacie said. "Any clues?"

"No, the scent stops right here, in the middle of the yard.

We need to do circles and try to find it again."

"Could all this moisture be interfering with Leo's ability to follow the scent?"

"No, it seems to help. When there's high moisture content in the air, it traps and holds scents close to the ground."

"We'll get out of your way," Pacie said, turning around.

"Where did the scent go, I wonder," Irma said.

"I don't know. It stopped nowhere near the road. There's nothing to climb up onto. And there's no river through the yard."

When they got in the SUV, Pacie looked at the dashboard clock. "It's two o'clock. Are you hungry? I don't think you've eaten anything all day."

"No, but Mr. Dibble probably is."

As if he knew what they were talking about, Mr. Dibble began dancing.

"I'll go through McDonald's drive-through and get a couple of burgers for him. Then we'll go to Sugar Sand Park." Pacie looked at Irma, watching her for any negative body language. Instead of protesting, she nodded in agreement.

"I just don't feel good; I feel on edge." Irma's hands shook as she reached for a cigarette. "I think it's a combination of the stress of these missing kids, the nightmares, and the sleep-walking—which I can't believe I'm doing."

"I know, me either." Pacie drove into the fast-food joint. "Thankfully, tomorrow is your sleep study and hopefully they'll come up with some answers about what's going on."

"I sure hope so."

Pacie drove up to the speaker and ordered a couple of plain

hamburgers and four bottles of water. When the attendant handed Pacie the food, she handed one of the water bottles to Irma. "Here, you have to stay hydrated."

Pacie pulled into the quiet park and opened the car's back hatch. She took out two dog bowls that she kept there for just such an occasion. She let Mr. Dibble out of the car and gave him one of the burgers, then poured water into a stainless-steel bowl. She walked over to Irma, still seated in the SUV with the door open. "You're not looking so good."

"As I said before, I don't feel good."

Pacie turned when she heard tires crunching gravel. "The lawn care guy is here. I'm gonna talk to him. I'll be right back."

Mr. Dibble followed Pacie to the truck and trailer loaded with lawnmowers and other equipment. Two young men got out of the truck. "Hi."

The one who had been driving paused, frowned, then said, "You look familiar. Do I know you?"

"I'm Pacie Rose. I was wondering if I could ask you a few questions."

He squinted as if the sun was shining in his eyes. "Oh, yeah, I know you. You're the lady that investigates weird stuff around town."

"That's me."

He extended a well-worn hand. "I'm Pete, Pete Chesson, owner of Quality Lawn Care, if you need to write that down. And that's my brother Donny."

"Thank you," Pacie said, typing it into her phone. "I'll let Irma know. But what I was wondering was if you guys have seen anything strange around here lately? I'm sure you know this park was where a young girl was recently abducted."

"Yeah, that was a terrible thing. But no, not that I can think of," Pete said. He turned to his brother, who was now standing near them. "Donny, have you seen anything strange around here?"

Donny shook his head. "No, but we don't maintain the trails, only the park's yard and this up here by the road."

Pete spit chewing tobacco onto the ground, just missing Mr. Dibble, who was sniffing around a tire. "Are you looking for anything in particular?"

"Any cult-like things or tulpamancy."

"What's tulpamancy?" Donny asked.

"It's creating a character or entity simply by using your mind. Kinda like having an imaginary friend, but ... real."

"How the hell is that done?" Pete said, shoving more chew into his cheek.

"I guess they meditate. They think about it, and talk to it until it talks back ... until it's conjured."

"Sounds like a mental illness to me." Donny laughed.

"Some say it's real. Some things you might find are candles, incense, stuff like that."

They both responded to the negative.

Pacie was about to walk back to Irma when she remembered a palace being mentioned in the journal. "Do you know of any mansions around here? Not the ones we all know about but hidden ones, that no one talks about? Maybe even something like a palace."

"There's no palace around here." Pete chuckled. "But as far as mansions, I assume you're not talking about the ones here in town and the museum."

"Yeah, a different one. Like one around the park, maybe."

They thought a moment, then Pete said, "I've never seen it, but there's a rumor that there used to be a mansion back in those very woods." He pointed toward the area where Morgan was taken.

"Tell me about it."

"The rumor goes that you're not even supposed to talk about it or bad things will come your way." Pete spit again. "That's probably why few people have heard of it."

"It's only a rumor, Pete," Donny said. "But there's supposed to be an old mansion back in those woods that was built a long time ago. There isn't even a road or trail to it. It's probably not even standing anymore. But it's said that if you happen to find the mansion, that you won't come back. That there's a guy who lives there who will hold you prisoner and torture you. And no one has ever escaped from it. I even tried to find it when I was a kid, but the woods are thick and I got scared when I thought someone was following me. So I ran out."

"Like a chicken," Pete said.

"At least I'm still here," Donny said.

Pacie thought for a moment. "I think I might've heard about that place, but as you said, no one talks about it. It's forgotten."

"Almost forgotten," Donny said.

"Do you think I could find it?" Pacie pulled up a map of the area on her phone. "Can you show me where you think it's at?"

Donny took her phone. He drew a circle near the screen with his finger. "If I remember correctly, it's in this area. Can

I turn on the satellite layer?"

"Sure."

With Pete looking over his shoulder, Donny said, "Yeah, like I thought, there's no sign of a mansion anywhere, not even a house or road. But I wouldn't go back there if I were you. The forest can be hard to walk through and there could be snakes and stuff."

Donny handed her back the phone. She studied the area where he had pointed to. There was no sign that anyone had ever lived in that location.

"Is that all?" Pete said, inching toward the trailer of mowers. "We gotta get to work."

"Yeah, that's all. Thank you for your help," Pacie said.

Mr. Dibble ran up to Irma ahead of Pacie. He wagged his tail as Irma petted him, leaning from the passenger seat.

"Well, I have some additional information," Pacie said, leaning against the open door.

"No."

"No?"

"I couldn't hear everything you were talking about, but I can't do it."

"I understand," Pacie said, watching Irma hang her head. "Remember how a mansion was mentioned in the journal?"

Irma straightened up. "Yeah."

"Well, rumor has it that there's an old mansion somewhere back in those woods, but no one's seen it. It wasn't even visible on the satellite view."

"Maybe it's a rumor."

"Now I know you're sick because you're not jumping to

investigate it."

Irma looked at Pacie with tired eyes. "You would be right on that."

"Let's get you back to my place so you can rest. I'll even make you chicken noodle soup."

"Good idea."

Pacie opened the backseat door. "Hop in, Mr. Dibble. We're going home."

After arriving home, Pacie made Irma the agreed-upon chicken noodle soup with a bottle of cold water. She placed it on a cafeteria tray with a cloth napkin and took it upstairs to Irma's bedroom.

"Are you going to be okay if I leave for a while?" Pacie asked.

Irma stopped unscrewing the cap on the water and looked at Pacie. "What are you going to do? Not looking for that mansion, I hope."

"I do want to check it out. There's probably no such thing, and I'm wasting my time."

Irma took a swallow of water. "I'm going to text Haley and see if she's ever heard of that mansion."

"Let me know what she says," Pacie said, walking toward the door.

"Text me every half hour so that I know you're okay," Irma said as she took her phone from the nightstand. "It's four now, so I'll expect a text around four-thirty. And it's probably a good idea to do some live recording so that I can watch you on the website."

"Will do." Pacie waved as she walked out the door. She grabbed a can of mosquito spray and drove back to the park.

The fog had lifted a bit, but it still refused to release its grip on Black Water.

Pete and Donny had gone, having finished manicuring the landscape. Pacie sent Irma a text that she was at the park. She looked at the satellite view once again. There was an area in the forest that had fewer trees, but no signs of a building. "I'll see if I can find that area."

Pacie opened the center console to get her Black Water Blue Stars baseball cap, but it was not there. Then she remembered it was in the backseat, now trampled and dirty from Mr. Dibble walking on it. "Oh, well. At least it'll keep the bugs off my head."

She got out of the car, snugged the cap onto her head, and walked to the trail that was still lined with yellow police tape. She ducked under it and walked down the path. Darkness replaced the fog. No, not replaced the fog, transformed the fog to an ash gray. As she walked into it, she could see things near her, but the distance was cloudy.

She walked to the fork in the trail and turned left. Pacie thought of recording the video but thought it best to wait until she got closer. She did not want to run down her battery too soon. She kept a power pack in her purse that would charge her phone a couple of times, but she would save its juice for now.

Mosquitoes and deer flies were swarming around her. She took the bug spray from her satchel and sprayed herself from head to foot. These pests might be the enemies that cause her to retreat. For now, she would continue ahead.

When she reached the hill leading down into the gully, she stopped and looked at the map. Deciding to stay on the high ground, she left the trail at this point. She sent Irma a text to let her know what she was doing.

Pacie found a spot almost free of raspberry thorns and walked off the trail. She looked at the map again and walked in the direction that she thought would take her to the clearing. Her phone dinged. Irma had sent her a text.

Be careful.

I am, she texted back.

Pacie pushed her way through brambles that kept wanting to tangle up her feet. Having almost fallen a few times, she looked around. There had to be a better way through this. If there was a mansion in here, then the vegetation was doing a good job of guarding the perimeter. It was slow going, but she kept pushing forward.

After an hour or so, she finally saw the forest beginning to thin. She had to be close to her destination. Pacie looked at the map and saw that she had made it. All she had to do was to get through the current bunch of brambles and she would be free to walk without being continuously scratched.

When she finally broke free of the clawing brush, she felt relieved. Until she thought about the daunting task of having to walk back through it to get to the trail. She needed to find a better way out.

Pacie looked at the map. The nearest roads were far away. She would check the clearing and if there were no signs of a mansion or debris, she would turn around. Especially since searchers had surely walked this area yesterday.

The air felt heavy on her chest as if a vice grip were clamping it. She texted Irma. *I'm almost to the clearing. I'll record soon. Going to make the video private. Don't want kids coming out here if it's dangerous.*

Irma texted back. *Ok. I'll edit it and make parts of it public later.*

Then she heard a branch snap. Pacie looked in the sound's direction and saw nothing but the eerie darkness that filled distant spaces. Fearing the worst, she began live recording. She turned the phone in the sound's direction and when she saw nothing to worry about, she began walking ahead. If there was a mansion, she would know soon.

When Pacie went through the last line of trees, she had reached the clearing. The dark fog made it difficult to see far, but she was sure she saw a structure. When she got closer, she saw an outline of a building. It was enormous. It was a mansion.

Chapter 11

HOW WAS IT POSSIBLE that this massive building did not appear on the satellite image? It was old, really old. While not as grandeur as her mansion, it had probably been built around the time of the civil war. It was around way before satellites. Had someone purposely erased it out of the images? If so, why? It had to be because they did not want anyone coming back here.

But Pacie was here. If the rumor was true, then she had set herself up to be cursed, at least according to the lawn care guys. But that was not her primary concern; she wanted to find the missing children. This place had to be where they were taken. But if they were being held captive inside, the searchers would have reported it. But there had been no news to that effect.

The three-story building was in disrepair. Even the few trees immediately surrounding it looked—dead. Shutters were dangling from windows. Vines clung to the exterior, seeming to keep the mansion's bones from breaking apart or to dissolve it into a fermenting glob. And the turret reinforced the impression that someone was watching her from one of the tower windows. But no one appeared to be living there.

Deciding it was best to walk around the mansion to see if anyone was there, she silenced her phone and quietly made her way around the house. She did not see any cars or useable paths to even get to it. Although there was what appeared to be an old driveway, it was now filled with mature trees. The only people she could imagine living there would be the homeless, but even that seemed unlikely. Nevertheless, Pacie could feel eyes upon her.

Irma kept texting her, but she ignored them for now. She had to stay focused. But if kids were inside that house, they were being awfully quiet. As far as she could tell, the mansion had been abandoned years ago, allowing sumac and shrubs to claim and obscure any signs of human activity. It was as though the building had been plopped into its spot by a giant ogre playing with toys.

Pacie was approaching the once grand entrance and the stone steps leading to the columnar portico when her phone vibrated, indicating the battery was getting low. She stopped recording and looked at her messages.

Haley said the building was searched, and they found nothing, Irma's latest text said.

Pacie reached into her satchel and brought out the power pack. While her phone was recharging, she texted back. *I stopped recording because my battery is low. I see no one. I'll go inside soon and look around.*

Irma texted, *Haley said not to bother with it and to turn around and come back.*

Why?

*I guess because they already searched it and the structure
could be unsafe.*

Oh.

Are you safe? Should I call Johnny?

*No, I'm fine. It's already been searched, so there's likely
nothing here.*

Pay better attention to your texts, please!

Sorry, I silenced the phone just in case someone was here.

Don't be long, it will be dark soon.

Just a quick check, then I'll head back.

Start recording before you go inside.

Okay, but I'm not at full charge.

Pacie kept her phone plugged into the power pack and
began recording as she climbed the stone steps to the portico.
The columns supporting the roof looked solid. The people
who had built the structure years ago were certainly skilled in
their trade, even taking time to carve ornate details into the
wooden brackets supporting the eaves.

The double entry door was closed, so she walked to a
nearby window and peered inside. The glass was hazy, making
it difficult to see anything. But a window farther down the
porch had a missing section of glass that left a small open area
to look through.

It was dark inside, but she could see covered furniture. It
surprised her this home from the past had not been ransacked
by hooligans.

"Hello," Pacie said through the window. "Is anyone in
there?"

It was silent, so she walked back to the front door. There

was no sense in using the lion's head doorknocker, so she turned the cast-metal doorknob. Pacie had to use her shoulder and body weight to force the door open. Little light spilled into the interior from the setting sun and the obstructive forest trees outside. She would need to inspect the place quickly; otherwise, she would need to walk back to her car in the dark.

Not wanting to use any more of her phone's battery than necessary, Pacie took a small flashlight from her purse, tapped it a few times to stop the flickering, and shined it around the interior. There were cobwebs everywhere—on the chalky furniture slipcovers, hanging from the chandelier in the foyer, and dangling from the corners of the wall and ceiling. But what perplexed her was the thick layer of dust on the hardwood floor. No one had disturbed it. There were no footprints or shuffle marks of any kind. If the search crew had checked the mansion, no one went inside. Why? It did not look that dangerous. The floor looked stable, with no missing floorboards exposing the basement. In fact, with some elbow grease, a lot of elbow grease, a person could live there if they wanted to. What was up with this place? Were the searchers afraid to go inside?

Pacie, however, was not afraid to go inside. Still recording, she said into the microphone, "It doesn't look like anyone has searched inside, so I'm going to check it out."

You're adding to my stress level, Pacie, Irma said in the online comments.

"Sorry."

Pacie stepped over the threshold and into the entryway. Other than a creak or two, the floor seemed secure. She looked down and saw her footprints in the dust. Had Haley outright lied to Irma about the house being searched?

After holding back three sneezes, she steadied the phone. "I'm gonna have to move fast before it gets dark. But I don't think there are any kids in here." Pacie looked at the phone's red-colored battery icon. It did not want to charge. "I'm going to stop recording so that I can get my phone charged."

Ok, but keep your phone on.

"Will do."

Pacie stopped recording, made sure the charger was connected securely and placed it in her satchel. She thought about going upstairs, but when she heard nearby coyotes howling, she knew it was best to get out of the woods and back to civilization before she had to spend the night inside what looked like a classic haunted house.

But Pacie had come this far. It would not be right to leave without giving the place at least a cursory inspection. She imagined a child tied up and gagged somewhere in the mansion, and decided it was more important to do a quick search rather than leave because of the dark. She could not live with herself if that was the case.

With the flashlight in hand, Pacie walked into the kitchen. There was an old cast-iron cookstove, a deep sink with a wraparound skirt, and a wooden table that no one had sat at for years. She walked up to the icebox and opened it. As expected, there was no food inside, aside from something that was way past the mold stage of decay.

"Johnny, you'd love this place," Pacie said aloud. "I wonder who owns it; maybe the state does."

Pacie walked throughout the first floor, shining her light

into the rooms. The only footprints she saw were hers in the dust. At the back of the house was a secondary staircase leading upstairs, but she would use the primary one because it was wider, and she could see better. As she walked back to the entrance, she wondered what the mansion looked like when people actually lived there. It had to have been beautiful. There were several fireplaces and decorative plaster ceilings in some rooms. Even the mantles above the fireplaces still had items like oil lamps and other dust-covered objects. If she had time, she would love to go through the house and imagine what it used to be like to live there.

"I think I want to buy this place," she said as she stood at the bottom of the staircase. But then she thought of all the work it would take to update it. Especially since she still had lots of renovations to do on her current house. Did it even have electricity? She shined her light on the wall and saw a push-button light switch. The mansion must have been updated in the early nineteen-hundreds when electricity came to the area. Did it have gas lamps before that? Pacie had no idea, but Johnny would know.

Pacie faced the shadowy staircase before her. The house and the outdoors were darker than when she first came inside. It was too late to turn back now; she was going to have to walk back to the park in the dark with the coyotes. Fortunately, coyotes were afraid of humans and would stay away, but with all of Black Water's strangeness, who knew what these coyotes were like. They ate things from mice, all the way up to deer. If they can take down a deer, they could take her down.

Pacie stepped onto the first step and then the next. Each

one creaked yet felt walkable below her feet. When she reached the second floor, she shined her light left and right down the hallway.

"Guess I'll go left first." Some doors were open, and some were closed. She would need to check every room. Many were empty, while others had a bed and dresser. "I'm for sure bringing Johnny out here."

When she reached the end of the hallway, she felt like sitting on one of the chairs in what was basically a rounded sitting area. She shined her flashlight out the window, into the forest.

Pacie jumped, almost dropping her light. Was that a person she saw standing among the trees? Not really wanting to, for fear of seeing that person again, she shined her light back to where she had seen someone standing. She was relieved she did not see it, but she knew what she saw and there was someone out there.

Chapter 12

IT WAS FOGGY AND dark outside. What she saw had to be a tree trunk in the shape of a human, she told herself.

"What do I do now?" she whispered, shining her flashlight back down the hallway toward the staircase. If it was a person standing outside watching her, was it the kidnapper? Or something more innocent, like a kid wanting to camp out there for the night? If it was the kidnapper, she would need to run out of the house or hide somewhere. If it was something nonthreatening, she would stay alert and continue investigating. But more than likely it was her eyes playing tricks on her. She would finish searching and then get the hell out of there.

Pacie walked quickly down the rest of the hallway and checked all the rooms. There was nothing to find. Then she moved up to the third floor. It had fewer rooms, but they were large, with high ceilings and open floor plans. "This must be the party floor."

Next was the turret. Pacie smiled when she saw two tapestry chairs with a small table between them inside the small tower. The nook would be the perfect place for an office or reading area. A chandelier hung from the cone roof, and windows circled the tower walls.

Except for the basement and attic, Pacie had checked most of the mansion. There was no sign of anyone having been there, not even the search group. Now it was time to go, but first she would check her phone. She sat in one of the turret chairs and unplugged her phone from the charger. There were a few messages from Irma asking how she was doing and had she left and where she was, along with a couple of voicemails.

Pacie called Irma.

"It's about time," Irma said, not bothering with a greeting. "Are you still at the mansion?"

"I'm still at the mansion, but I'm going to leave when I'm done talking to you. I'm in the tower right now."

"Tower?"

"Yeah, this used to be a nice place, but now it's a rundown building. But the kids aren't here. I've searched most of it."

"Okay, now get out of there," Irma said. "I was about to call Johnny and go looking for you."

"It'll take me over an hour to get back through the woods, though. I'm not looking forward to that."

"This is a rather foolish thing you've done. You should've left earlier and taken someone with you," Irma said. "But I am relieved that you didn't find anything. I was afraid Slenderman was holding you captive."

"Not yet."

"What do you mean, not yet?"

"Nothing. I'll see you soon." Pacie did not want to worry Irma, else she would send Johnny to come to her rescue.

Pacie put the phone in her back pocket and walked down the staircase to the second-floor landing. She stopped when she heard sounds coming from the first floor. It sounded like something walking around. Then she remembered she had left the front door open; an animal could have wandered inside.

When Pacie got to the point in the staircase where she could shine her light downstairs, she noticed she had indeed left the door ajar. She stopped moving when she saw a coyote looking up at her. Its eyes glowed red. Was that normal for a coyote or a sign that this was a devil dog?

It stood there, staring up the staircase as if deciding whether to charge her or turn around and leave through the door. Then Pacie remembered she had read that to scare coyotes you should make loud noises. She clapped her hands and shouted, "Get out of here. Go! Go!"

To her relief, it did. And so did two others who ran out of the living room. "Glad that worked."

Pacie walked down the steps and out the front door. She closed it tight behind her just as she had found it. While she stood on the portico, she shined her light around the perimeter for that man, and to figure out the direction she had come from earlier.

I'm leaving the house now, Pacie texted Irma.

The beam of her flashlight was bright, but it had difficulty penetrating the fog. Nothing looked familiar. "Great, I'm gonna get lost."

Pacie opened the map on her phone and set the park as her walking destination. It showed her a dotted line to follow, but it seemed wrong. Like its compass was being pulled off course by a magnetic anomaly. But she had no choice, her best bet was to follow it. And so she would.

When she had walked a short distance, she turned around and shined the light back through the mist toward the mansion. Was that a human standing at the front door? She could not tell for sure. The only thing that Pacie knew was that she was not walking back, she was running.

Running through the thickets was not possible, but she could move at a fast pace. Pacie would trip, catch her balance, and trip again. She maintained the forward momentum for a while until an unforgiving raspberry vine caught Pacie's ankle and made her fall to the damp ground. Her phone flew from her hand.

"Where is it?" Pacie said, panicked. She wished she had never come here. She had accomplished nothing, other than knowing that no kids were being held captive in the mansion.

"There you are," she said, catching sight of the screen's glow. Thorns scratched the skin of her hands when she reached inside the bush.

Pacie stood up and looked at the phone's navigation. It showed she was off course. How could that be? She looked up at the sky, hoping to see the lights of town or the power plant that would help guide her. But the forest was dense, and the fog seemed to scatter any light she saw, so she followed the map.

Moving too fast through the woods was not good for her face. Low branches would smack her cheeks, and she feared one would find an eye to poke.

"This is going to be a long night," Pacie said, stopping for a rest and to get her bearings straight. She was lost; there was no doubt. Every time she checked the map, it said she was going the wrong way.

An hour had passed and Pacie still had not found the trail that would take her back to town. She hoped she could hear sounds like car engines or waves crashing, but there were no sounds other than her breathing. It was just like at Anna's house, where young Seth was kidnapped. The fog was absorbing sound waves.

"Ah, it looks like the trees are thinning," Pacie said, hoping the path was just ahead.

Pacie tripped and fell for the hundredth time. After cussing a moment, she looked up. She could not believe it. She had walked in a circle back to that damned mansion.

Chapter 13

IRMA PACED AROUND THE spacious blue room. She had found a figure-eight path that suited her anxious steps. It allowed her to pace around the canopy bed repeatedly as she moved nervously from fireplace to desk, occasionally parting the curtains to see if car lights were driving toward the house. She heard the downstairs grandfather clock as it chimed the midnight hour. Pacie was not answering her texts or voicemails. Something was wrong. She wanted to call Johnny, but it was so late.

"I don't know what to do, Mr. Dibble. I'm sure Johnny won't mind if I call him. I should've called him earlier. I'd check on Pacie myself but I don't have my car. It's too far to walk home in the dark and there's a bad guy out there anyway. What do I do?"

Mr. Dibble, who had been watching her from his resting spot on the cushioned chair, continued to follow her with his eyes as she kept walking back and forth.

"I have to call Johnny. There's no other choice."

Irma picked up her phone from the nightstand and

hesitated only a moment before calling. The phone kept ringing, soon to go to voicemail.

"Hello."

Irma could tell she woke him up. "Johnny, this is Irma. I'm sorry to bother you so late, but Pacie hasn't come home. I think something's wrong."

There was shuffling in the background as if he were sitting up in bed. "What? Where is she?"

"She's at Sugar Sand Park. She went looking for a mansion in the woods, and she found it. She said she was heading back. That's when I lost contact with her. I was thinking you could pick me up and we could head over there. I'm at Pacie's house."

"I'll be right over," Johnny said with a grunt as if standing up. "Someday you two have got to stop these investigations and leave them to the police where they belong."

Irma could tell he was not happy. Especially since it was not the first time he had said that to her. "Okay. Bye."

She went up to her bedroom and brought down her backpack. Fumbling with her keyring, she said, "Where is the house key?"

Mr. Dibble was already waiting by the door.

"I think this one is it." Irma turned on the porch light and she and Mr. Dibble stepped outside. Irma tried to lock the door, but the key would not go in the lock. "Damn it."

After trying a couple of other keys on the ring, she was back at the first one. It worked this time. "I must not have been doing it right."

It was not long before Johnny pulled into the driveway. Irma and Mr. Dibble climbed into the pickup. Mr. Dibble first claimed the middle spot in the front seat, but Johnny shooed him to the backseat of the club cab.

"Thanks for doing this," Irma said.

"When was the last time you talked to her?" Johnny said, pulling onto the street.

Irma looked at her phone. "An hour or two ago."

"You said she found a mansion back there?"

"She did, and I even have the video."

"I want to see it when there's time. The only mansion I know that was back there is long gone. It belonged to a wealthy ship captain. His name was Captain Perry. He didn't have any heirs, so when he died the house was left unoccupied and eventually fell into disrepair. I think the state tore it down."

"It's still there. Pacie found it."

Johnny pulled into the park and stopped next to Pacie's SUV. "This weather has really been something. She's probably lost in the dark with all this fog."

"And her phone's battery is more than likely dead," Irma said, opening her car door.

"Wait, what are you doing?"

"We're going to look for her, aren't we?"

Johnny took a flashlight from the glove compartment. "*I'm* going to look for her. You are going to stay here and blow the horn now and then. I'm hoping Pacie will hear it and follow it."

"I'll be waking up the neighbors and I'm sure the police will be called."

Johnny laid on the horn before he climbed out of the truck. "Well, if they do come out, they can help search for Pacie."

"Oh, wait," Irma said, sliding across the seat. She opened the map on her phone. "I think this clearing here is where she went."

"I think that is where the captain's mansion was, but I'm sure I also heard that it was demolished years ago." Johnny opened the map on his phone. "Keep your phone handy in case I need to call you."

Irma nodded. "Do you want to take Mr. Dibble with you? He'll protect you."

Johnny watched the dog dance and move toward the door as if he were going to let him out. "I'm good. Just keep blowing the horn every minute or so."

Irma watched Johnny walk into the grass and then disappear into the dense fog. She blew the horn twice.

"Johnny will find her," Irma said, motioning for Mr. Dibble to join her in the front seat. "Or he just might come up missing, too."

Chapter 14

PACIE STOOD MOTIONLESS, STARING at the massive structure. It looked different. It looked newer, but she could not tell
for sure. She did not want to get closer to it but the shutters
she could see were not dangling; they were in their proper
places on the windows. She looked at her phone. The screen
was dark, and it would not turn on. She took the charger from
her satchel and plugged it into the phone, but it too had no
power. "Great."

Her flashlight still worked, so Pacie turned around and
did her best guess as to the direction she was to go. She knew
Irma would tell Johnny she was missing. That at least brought
a little comfort to her as she walked at a slow pace toward what
she hoped was civilization. But what unnerved her were the
coyote howls. They seemed to be getting closer.

Through the brambles and over rotting logs, she trudged.
It felt like she was going in a straight line. If so, she would come
out to a trail, a road, or something at some point. "That stupid
map is what made me go in a circle."

Her nerves tingled with pain when she heard a nearby

huff and the movement of animals around her. It had to be those coyotes. They were following her. Pacie shined her light around, glimpsing their beady red eyes. She groaned. How was she going to get out of this?

Pacie clapped her hands and shouted at them. It worked last time at the house, but this time they are not as intimidated by her. She wanted to run, but she assumed that if she did, they would likely attack her, like the canines they were.

But her forward movement came to an abrupt stop when the coyotes had her surrounded. She made more noise to scare them away, but it was not working.

"Go on, get away from me," she yelled while feeling around inside her satchel for the pocketknife. Where was it? But what did it matter? If she was attacked by a half-dozen coyotes, the knife would do little to help her.

Then Pacie heard what she thought was someone calling her name. Johnny?

"I'm over here. Can you hear me?"

"Pacie. I'm on my way. Keep talking."

Her talking was shouting at the coyotes who were backing away. When Johnny came through the wall of mist with his flashlight shining on her, she ran toward him. "Oh my god, you just saved my life. I was surrounded by coyotes and they acted like they were about to attack me."

Johnny held her while he shined his light around the area. "I don't see any, they must've run away."

Pacie would not let him release her hand as they walked toward the distant blowing horn.

"Did you hear the horn blowing?" Johnny asked.

"No, not until now. This fog has a way of dampening sounds."

"I've never heard of that before. Are you feeling alright?" Johnny laughed.

"Hilarious," Pacie said, nudging him. "There's nothing wrong with me—that I know of."

"Oh, so you're not one hundred percent positive as to the state of your mental health?"

Pacie could not see his face clearly in the darkness, but she knew he was smiling. "Sometime soon I want to show you the mansion I found. That's where I was at."

"The state tore the old captain's mansion down a long time ago. You found some other house."

"Well, I don't know whose house it was, but it was three stories high with a tower and in fairly decent shape for being, what looked like, from the eighteen-hundreds."

Johnny stopped walking. "That sounds like the captain's mansion. I guess I'm wrong, they must not have demolished it." He held his phone for her to see the screen. "But if that's the case, why isn't it on this map?"

"That's what I've been trying to figure out."

They finally reached the trail and followed it to the park. Irma began tapping the horn with a welcoming melody.

"She's going to wake up the entire neighborhood," Pacie said. "You'd better tell her she can stop blowing the horn."

Mr. Dibble ran up and greeted them as they approached.

Irma jumped out of the pickup and hugged Pacie. "Thank god you're alright. I thought something bad had happened to you."

"Almost. Johnny rescued me in a nick of time."

"Okay, you two. Let's go home," Johnny said. "Let's get some sleep and talk about it later."

Pacie unlocked her car and let Mr. Dibble inside. While Irma walked around to the passenger side, Johnnie put his arms around her. "Thank you for coming to my rescue."

Johnny kissed her. "Like I told your cuz, you need to stop doing these investigations."

Pacie said nothing. Instead, she kissed him for longer than she should have.

Irma laid on the car horn and shouted. "Either get a room or let's get going. I have a sleep study later today. I need to get my beauty sleep."

Chapter 15

PACIE PUT ON HER light pajamas and walked to Irma's room. Both Mr. Dibble and Irma were already snoring. She closed the guestroom door and walked to her bedroom. It felt so good to crawl under the sheet. She was exhausted. Sleep would come fast.

With a start, Pacie opened her eyes. Was it a dream or did a noise wake her up? She listened. The doors to her bedroom were partway open, allowing her to hear sounds. It must be Irma using the downstairs bathroom or finding something to eat. She looked at the clock, it was four in the morning. They had not been to sleep that long. She closed her eyes, then opened them back up when she remembered Irma saying she had been sleepwalking.

Pacie sat on the side of the bed; she had better check on Irma. It sounded like she was going through kitchen drawers. She must be looking for the silverware.

Pacie was about to stand up and go see what Irma was doing when she heard the click of Mr. Dibble's nails coming up the main staircase. It surprised her when she noticed the steps were walking toward her bedroom. Pacie looked toward her partially closed bedroom door. She saw it slowly open. Irma was standing there. Standing there and looking in her direction. Mr. Dibble was at her side.

"Is everything alright?" Pacie asked, expecting Irma to talk about the inconvenient mansion, but instead, she did not answer.

Pacie turned on the lamp as Mr. Dibble walked into the room. Then she saw it. Irma was holding a butcher knife in her hand. It was obvious Irma was sleepwalking, but why did she have a knife? "Irma?"

Irma stepped into the room. Pacie stood up next to the bed. In her mind, she thought she could probably overtake Irma and make her drop the knife, but she was not sure. She had a gun in the nightstand drawer, but there was no way she would use it on her cousin.

"Irma, wake up." Pacie clapped her hands like she had done with the coyotes.

Irma stood there with vacant, wide-open eyes. "I can't kill. I can't kill."

Who was she talking to? "Irma, it's me, Pacie."

Irma stepped closer; now only four or five feet away from Pacie. Mr. Dibble began barking.

Pacie's heart raced. "Irma, drop the knife."

Instead of dropping it, Irma raised it. That's when Mr. Dibble jumped, thrusting himself into Irma's chest, causing her to lose her balance and fall backward.

Pacie saw the knife slide across the floor. She ran and picked it up.

Mr. Dibble began licking Irma's face.

"What is going on? Get off of me," Irma said, pushing the dog away.

Pacie sat the knife on the bed and then knelt beside her. "Irma, are you okay?"

Irma wiped the drool from the side of her mouth and groaned as she sat up. She looked around the room. "How did I get in here?"

"You were sleepwalking again. Do you feel well enough to stand?"

"I think so."

Pacie helped Irma to the edge of the bed. "Sit here a moment."

"Oh my god," Irma said, looking at the knife. "Don't tell me I was carrying that."

"Do you remember anything?"

Irma rubbed her forehead. "It was the man. Slenderman. He's in my head and telling, no demanding that I do things. I'm so sorry, Pacie. I would never do anything to hurt you."

Pacie sat next to Irma and put an arm around her shoulder. "I know. Your sleep study is tonight. Hopefully, the doctor can fix what's going on."

"I don't think it's a problem a doctor can fix," Irma said as tears began streaming down her cheeks.

"If Slenderman is causing this, I think the key is somewhere in that mansion," Pacie said. "But I didn't find anything there. No signs of people or kids or Slenderman."

'I want to go out there with you tomorrow," Irma said, standing up quickly. She winced with pain and sat back down.

"There's something there, we're just missing it."

Pacie said nothing for a moment. She worried Irma was becoming obsessed with this entity that calls itself Slenderman. "Alright. We'll do it in the morning, tomorrow morning, so that we have plenty of sunlight. If the sun can break through this never-ending fog."

Irma looked at the bedside clock. "It's four-thirty. I don't think I want to go back to sleep."

"I'll get a pot of coffee going," Pacie said, standing up. "Can you walk, or do I need to call the doctor? Mr. Dibble did a good job at knocking you down."

Irma stood up, stooped, and held her hip. "I'm getting old, Pacie."

Pacie laughed. "I know, you look like it."

"You didn't have to agree with me." Irma shuffled toward the door. "Can you get my cigarettes?"

"That's part of your problem. Smoking's going to kill you one way or the other."

"I'm trying to quit."

"I know you are," Pacie said, following her into the hallway. "Maybe you should try hypnosis."

"Sounds like a bad idea. I don't want to get any closer to that Slenderman hiding in my head."

Chapter 16

"I'M STILL SORE FROM Mr. Dibble knocking me over," Irma said as she and Pacie walked into Black Water General Hospital that Monday evening.

"Want me to get you a wheelchair?" Pacie teased.

"Ha, ha," Irma said, hobbling toward the elevators.

Pacie laughed. "I wasn't kidding."

The sound of a male yelling from the direction of the emergency room offset the low-key nature of the hospital's main lobby. It was not that people were anxiety-free, but instead, they seemed hesitant and paranoid of others around them.

Irma walked into the empty elevator. "I think the child abductions and this eerie weather have people on edge."

"No doubt. I'm even feeling a little on edge myself," Pacie said, looking at the panel of buttons. "The third floor?"

"That's right," Irma said, looking at the email she had printed out.

"Are you sleepy?" Pacie asked as she sat the suitcase on the elevator floor.

"I don't know what I am," Irma said. "Just don't tell them

about what happened this morning."

"They might need to know that information."

"They might use it to send me to the lockdown unit."

The elevator door opened. They followed the signs until they reached the Sleep Disorder Unit. They walked through the door and up to the front desk.

"Hi, I'm Irma Foster. I have a sleep study scheduled for nine o'clock."

The woman at the desk looked down at a book. "Welcome, Ms. Foster. Please fill out this sleep habit questionnaire and I'll take you to your room."

Irma took the clipboard and pen and sat in one of the waiting room chairs. "I need a cigarette."

"Have the doctor give you a nicotine patch or something."

"I don't know if that'll work."

Irma filled out the paperwork and returned it to the desk. When she sat back down, she rifled through the magazines sitting on the table next to her. "Automotive and retirement stuff. There's nothing I'm interested in."

Moments later, the young woman walked up to them. "My name's Amy. Please follow me. You'll be in Room Four."

Irma and Pacie followed Amy down a short hallway, turning right into an open area that had a room with large windows at the far end and two rooms on either side. Irma's room was on the left. It looked like a simple three-star hotel room.

After Amy gave a quick orientation of the equipment and call light, she said, "You can change into your pajamas. The technician will be with you shortly."

Pacie watched Amy close the door as she left the room.

Then she sat in a cushioned chair next to the bed. "This room isn't that bad."

Irma looked around at the drab navy curtains, fake flowers on a small table, and the more than likely hard mattress of the single bed. "There's no TV, and a camera is staring at me. I don't think I'll be able to go to sleep."

"I don't think you'll have a problem sleeping," Pacie said. "You haven't had much sleep lately. I'm sure you'll conk right out."

Irma took her pajamas out of the suitcase and went into the bathroom and changed.

Pacie giggled when Irma came out dressed in Daffy Duck pajamas. "Those are interesting PJ's. Why are you wearing them?"

"I knew you were going to say something," Irma said. "These were clean."

There was a knock at the door.

"Come in," Irma said, sitting on the edge of the bed.

"Hi, my name's Kim. I'm your technician tonight," a middle-aged woman said as she wheeled a computer into the room.

"Nice to meet you. I'm Irma," she said, fidgeting. "Do you think I can have a nicotine patch?"

"No problem," Kim said. "I have a few questions to ask you, then I'll put the sensors on your head, chest, and legs. And a clip on your ear."

"I don't know if I'll be able to sleep with all those things attached to me."

"They're important because they check brain waves, eye

movements, your breathing, and heart rate. It also checks your body movements."

Irma nodded. She knew all this. "Is someone going to be watching me all night?"

"We do. We watch you and listen to you, as well. So if you need to use the bathroom just speak to us and I'll come in and unhook you from the wires so that you can do that. There's also the call light if you need it."

"I've been sleepwalking," Irma said. She said it more as a safety warning rather than will they notice it. "Who's watching me when you're taking a break?"

"Victor will be watching. He's a technician, too, and we cover for each other when one of us goes on break," Kim said. Then she went through the admission assessment, entering the data into the computer.

"Do you have any other questions for me?" Kim asked.

"Will Doctor Plum be in tonight?"

"No, not unless he needs to. He rarely comes in until the morning."

Irma looked toward the door. "Is anyone else having a sleep study tonight?"

"Yeah, all our beds are full."

"Is that normal?"

"It happens, but I must say, it's been busier than normal lately."

Irma knew it was Slenderman causing people to have sleeping problems, but there was no way she was going to tell that to the tech. "That's all my questions."

"Okay. I'll bring you a nicotine patch and then get you

hooked up to the monitors," Kim said, leaving the room.

Pacie yawned. "It might not be that bad here. You'll be able to catch up on your sleep and find out what's been going on with you."

Irma exhaled. "I'm glad this is only one night."

Kim came back into the room with the patch and then attached Irma to the sensors and wires. Some plugged into a box that lay on the bed next to her, and others connected directly to the wall at the head of the bed.

Pacie stood up. "Now that you're tucked into bed, I'm going to head out. I don't know about you, but I'm going to sleep like a rock."

"I put you down as the emergency contact, so stay close to your phone."

"I will, but you know you're in one of the safest places you can be, especially with people watching your every move."

"Please, don't remind me."

Chapter 17

"I'M GONNA GET COFFEE, do you want some?" Victor said, resting his arms on the counter in front of the monitors; looking as though he was going to put his head down, like a student needing a nap in kindergarten.

Kim tilted her Styrofoam cup, watching the few drops of cold coffee roll around the bottom. "Yeah. I'm having trouble keeping my eyes open. I'm not used to working the night shift."

Victor looked at his watch. "It's around two and everyone's been quiet. Are you gonna be alright if I leave you here alone, newbie?"

"I think this newbie can handle it. What can happen in the few minutes you'll be gone?"

Victor shrugged. "I'll be right back."

Kim leaned back in her chair and stretched her arms over her head as Victor left the room. She looked at the black and white displays. The overweight man in Room 1 snored. A young woman in Room 2 periodically rolled from side to side. Room 3 had a frail elderly woman who did not move at all. Kim would have thought the old woman was dead if it were not for the monitor showing she was breathing. And Room 4 held Irma, who was snoring almost as much as the man in the room across the hall from her.

Kim was still charting her observations when Victor returned with the coffee.

"Any excitement while I was gone?" Victor sat a cup of coffee in front of Kim.

"No, just the usual boring stuff." Kim bent back the sipper lid and hesitantly tasted the coffee. "The machine must be failing; this isn't that hot."

Victor sat next to her. "You're right. But as long as it has caffeine, that's what's important."

Victor stared at Irma's screen. "Where's Room Four?"

"What?" Kim looked at the empty bed. "She probably went to the bathroom. I didn't hear anything from anyone."

"There was no alarm?"

"No. Maybe she knows how to silence it. I'll check on her."

Victor opened Irma's chart. "She's the one that has a history of sleepwalking, doesn't she?"

Kim nodded and left the lab. Aside from muffled snoring, the hallway was quiet. She knocked on Irma's door and then went inside. She flipped on the light switch and walked to the open bathroom door. Irma was not inside. She looked around the bedroom, in the closet, under the bed, and then at the camera. "She's not in here."

Victor called security to alert them that a patient might be sleepwalking. Then he met Kim in the hallway. "I called security. I didn't see her on the monitors in anyone's room, but I'll check them. You can look for her on the rest of the unit."

Kim's heart pounded, and she felt like she was going to pass out. She was new on the job and had already messed up by losing a patient. Where could Irma have gone? She had just checked the monitors moments earlier.

The hospital's public address system announced: CODE PURPLE SLEEP STUDY UNIT, CODE PURPLE SLEEP STUDY UNIT. Kim looked at the back of her ID badge. Sure enough, code purple announced the obvious, a missing patient.

Kim walked out of the observation area and checked the closed door on the right. It was the supply room filled with linens and towels. The light came on when she walked inside. Carts of sheets, bedspreads, and washcloths were against the wall. There was nowhere for the patient to hide. Kim looked behind the door and then walked out and around the corner to the reception area. No one was in the waiting room. She walked behind the desk. No one was hiding there. The patient had to of left the sleep study area.

Kim used the desk phone and called Victor. "She's not in the sleep study area. Did you find her?"

"No, she must've left the unit. Why don't you check the hallway, I'll stay here."

Kim walked out of the sleep study unit and into the hallway. Which way would a sleepwalker go?

A security guard walked off the elevator and up to Kim. "Did you find the missing patient?"

"No, I haven't. Victor probably told you she's a woman with gray hair, wearing pajamas with the Daffy Duck cartoon character on them. Her name's Irma."

The guard smiled. "He did. She should stand right out."

"I know." Kim blinked. She felt so irresponsible. "It happened so quickly. I was watching the monitors while Victor went for coffee. He wasn't gone that long."

The guard nodded reassuringly. "We'll find her. Any idea where she would've gone?"

"No idea, but she couldn't have gone far," Kim said. "We searched the entire unit, and she's not in there."

"Security has been alerted; she won't be able to leave the hospital. I'm going to talk to Victor."

"I'm gonna keep looking," Kim said, wiping her sweaty palms on her scrub pants.

Since the guard had come from the elevators on the left, Kim decided she would go down the corridor to the right. There was not much in that direction, just offices as far as Kim knew.

She walked quietly down the hallway, listening for movement. She tested the closed doors as she walked past them. They were all locked. At the end of the hallway was the exit, a stairwell. If the patient went this way, she would have had to use that door.

Kim opened the exit door. The stairwell went both up and down. There were no sounds of anyone climbing or descending the staircase. Which way would Irma have gone? There was one floor above her, but she had not been shown it during orientation. She thought she remembered the orienter say that the fourth floor was not used. That it was the old lockdown unit. Now it was storage.

Thinking security was checking the lower levels, expecting the patient to leave the hospital, she would go up to the fourth floor.

When Kim reached the top landing, there was a sign that read: LOCKED UNIT. BUZZ FOR THE ATTENDANT. She looked through the door's small window. The floor was dark. There was no way Irma would go in there—at least she hoped. But Kim had to find her missing patient, so she pulled on the door. It opened. She half wished the door was locked so that she could turn around and go back down to the unit with Victor.

"I've come this far, might as well check it out." Kim stepped inside and felt for light switches on the cold concrete wall. When she found them, she turned them on. Most of the lights that managed to come to life either flickered or cast a dim, gray glow. She switched them off and then back on, hoping the lighting would behave so that she could get a better view of the floor.

Kim took the small flashlight from her pocket, used for checking on patients in their dark rooms, and turned it on as she let the door close behind her. She stood in an antechamber with a nurses' station, encased in glass, directly ahead. There were three doors around the room, two of which were closed. The double doors directly ahead were propped open and revealed a long, darkened hallway with the same flickering lights. Stretchers and wheelchairs were haphazardly scattered along its length, devoid of anything that resembled a clean and healthy environment.

She walked up to the nurses' station and looked through the glass. Charts were still in the racks and paperwork was scattered on the desktop. It looked as though the old psychiatric unit had been abandoned quickly and no one ever bothered to go back and clean things up. Such disrespect for the patients' private medical records. Not to mention a waste of space. To Kim, it did not seem like the floor was being used for storage. But more like people had fled for their very lives.

There was a chill in the musty air. If Irma had come up here, she could be hiding anywhere.

The sound of something rolling at the far end of the main corridor caught Kim's attention. It had to be the patient. Irma had shown no signs of being violent and Kim knew sleepwalkers were typically harmless, but they could harm themselves. Some sleepwalkers have been known to drive a car, but fortunately, the patient likely did not have time to make it out to the parking lot.

Kim knew to speak in a quiet voice and to use a light touch to direct sleepwalkers back to bed. Otherwise, they could become confused and disoriented. When she found Irma, she would speak softly and guide her back to room four. Back to where it was not so creepy.

Kim saw a telephone on the counter. She would call Victor and let him know she was on the fourth floor, that she thought Irma was there, and to send a guard. She entered the nurses' station through the unlocked door and put the phone's handset to her ear. There was no dial tone. She clicked the hook a few times, but it made no difference. The phone was dead.

Not feeling any more confident with the self-talk of there being nothing to worry about, she walked from the nurses' station to the head of the long hallway. Lights continued to flicker, making it appear there was movement ahead of her.

Dark shadows spasmed along the corridor's length. The very end of the corridor was coal-black, and it was also where the sound of squeaking wheels was coming from.

"Irma," Kim said, sounding as non-threatening as possible, considering the anxiety she felt to leave the spooky floor was being reflected in her voice. "This is Kim. It's time to go back to your room."

Kim did not know if it was Irma down there or not, but who else could it be? She supposed it could be someone working, but who would do that in the middle of the night, on a vacant floor with not even a flashlight?

Kim's penlight did little to penetrate the darkness that fell before her, like a tarry tunnel to Hell.

Relax, Kim, relax, she told herself. *It's just an ordinary hallway with dark air. Nothing more, nothing less.*

Fortunately, the lights that were working gave Kim enough illumination to see where she was going. Paying little attention to the dark patient rooms on both sides of her, she focused on the end of the corridor where the sound was coming from. It was pitch black down there, but she could hear the intermittent squeal of what sounded like a wheelchair or a stretcher being moved. Not moved far, but far enough to get her attention.

Kim walked down the long, dimly lit hallway. Shining her light into rooms as she passed them. She imagined patients in their beds sleeping, but aside from bedframes with plastic-covered mattresses, and various pieces of furniture, like bedside tables, they were empty.

"Irma, it's Kim," she said, stopping so that she could hear

a response. But there was none.

Kim shivered as she continued to slowly walk down the hallway, forcing herself to continue toward what felt like would lead to her demise. The smell of a dead rat made her nose wrinkle. Then she saw, in the shadows at the end of the hall, what appeared to be someone sitting in a wheelchair, facing her. It freaked her out. She stopped and shined her light on it. She was far enough away that she could not tell if it was Irma, or someone else, but there was someone sitting still, very still. A dark object or shadow was cast over the top of the body; her light could not penetrate it. It sat motionless like a mannequin, not a person. Maybe someone thought it would be funny to place Resuscitation Annie in the wheelchair. That's all it was, an oversized doll.

"Irma, it's time to go back to your room." Kim did not want to get any closer. Something did not feel right. "Can you come to me, please? Let's go back downstairs."

The unusually dark shadows at the end of the corridor were like impenetrable objects themselves, stretching from floor to ceiling. The overhead lights, the ones that were working, did little to reveal the identity of the shapes. Eerily, any light there was, cast a dull spotlight on the torso of the body, as though wanting to draw attention to it.

This is a joke, Kim thought. Someone set this scene up on purpose as a prank. "This isn't funny."

Then there was the god-awful squeak of wheels needing to be oiled. Had the wheelchair moved? Kim was terrified. She froze in place, not sure whether to keep approaching the thing sitting still like a corpse or run back down the hallway.

One shadow in the corridor's corner moved, not from the flickering light but on its own. At least that's what it looked like to Kim. "If this is a joke, I'm not laughing."

Kim heard what sounded like a low, guttural sound. An animal? What animal could be in a hospital that could growl? Mice squeaked. Birds sang. But this sound was menacing. She wanted to turn around and run away. The guard could deal with it. But she had to redeem herself and safely return the patient to her room.

The light from Kim's penlight was weakening, and could barely penetrate the blackness before her, but she had to know for sure if it was Irma.

"Irma, it's time to go back to your room." Kim hesitantly moved closer to the body, wanting to see the pattern on the pajama bottoms. The pants were hospital-issued, not Daffy Duck. This was not Irma.

Kim could not move. She screamed when the body stood and moved toward her like a zombie. Its joints cracked like celery and twisted in unnatural angles.

The penlight fell from Kim's hand as she sprinted back down the hallway to the exit door. It would not open. She looked back and saw the disjointed corpse walking toward her. She screamed and was about to give up and find another way off the unit when a security guard opened the door.

"What's going on?" the guard asked as Kim rushed past him to the stairwell.

"Someone's coming after me," Kim said, standing on the landing, her arms crossed over her chest as if the horror of what she just experienced caused a deep freeze inside of her.

The guard shined his light around the anteroom and down the corridor. "Where? I don't see anything."

"In the hallway. It's coming down the hallway." Kim was still frantic.

"There's nothing there," he said. "Was it the patient?"

"No, someone else."

"I'll check it out."

Kim stood at the door, holding it open so that it would not lock the guard inside the unit. She looked down the hallway. There was no corpse coming for her. "It was there. A sick person was walking down the corridor. I swear. Maybe it went into a room."

The guard took his walkie-talkie from his belt. "Sam for Brian."

"Hey, Sam. Did you find her?"

"No, but there's a possible intruder on the fourth floor. I'm going to check it out. One of the sleep unit techs is with me."

"I'll be right up."

Sam replaced the walkie on his belt. "Brian's on his way to help search. You can go back down to the unit."

Kim nodded. "You should put something in the doorjamb to keep the door from closing because I couldn't get it to open."

Sam jingled the keys on his belt as he turned to walk toward the nurses' station. "I'll be fine."

Kim was about to leave, then turned back toward the guard. "Sam."

He turned toward her. "Yeah?"

"Be careful."

Chapter 18

Pacie could not move her legs. She was trapped in mud while the need to solve mathematical problems swirled in her head. Her boots slipped off her feet as she struggled to escape what was quickly turning into quicksand. Then a siren blasted. The enemy had found her and would soon spear her through the heart and leave her for the rabid dogs. But not before taking the rood treasure that she held in her hand.

When Pacie awoke, she knew she had just let out a stifled scream. She opened her hand as she reached for the ringing cellphone on the nightstand beside her bed. There was nothing in it.

"Hello." Pacie knew she sounded groggy. She glanced at the clock next to the lamp. It was two-thirty in the morning.

"May I speak with Pacie Rose, please?" The man said. "This is Victor, a tech from Black Water General Hospital."

Pacie jolted awake. "This is Pacie. Is Irma okay?"

"Well," Victor began. "Irma has apparently sleep-walked and...

"You can't find her?"

"We're looking for her. Security guards have sealed off the hospital, and I'm sure we'll find her soon."

"I'll be right there."

Pacie hung up and dressed quickly. She had set her clothes out just in case something like this happened. But how could this happen in the first place when Irma was being watched on camera?

Mr. Dibble was sleeping on an oversized stuffed chair next to Pacie's bed. "Come on, Mr. Dibble. You have to go outside."

The dog's head popped up, and he immediately jumped out of the chair and followed Pacie down the secondary staircase. Pacie held open the exterior door at the bottom of the steps, but Mr. Dibble just stood there looking out the opening toward the lake.

"Come on, go outside, Mr. Dibble." Pacie motioned with her arm. She finally had to give in and walk out onto the pillared piazza and into the yard to get him to follow. The grass was wet, and the fog still hung in the air. She looked up through the haze at the starless sky and then back down at Mr. Dibble who had accomplished the mission and was now sniffing around.

Pacie walked back inside. "You can come in now, Mr. Dibble."

The pooch ran through the doorway and into the study. When Pacie grabbed her satchel, Mr. Dibble was standing in the kitchen by the door to the garage.

"You have to stay here," she said. "You can't go with me inside the hospital."

Mr. Dibble sat down as if he knew exactly what she was

talking about, and he probably did.

Pacie patted the dog on the head and left the house. It made her feel uneasy and a little angry that the hospital could not find Irma. Where could she have gone?

The entire trip to the hospital had Pacie thinking of possibilities. More than likely, the minute she stepped into the sleep study unit, Irma would be back in bed. Safe and sound.

When Pacie reached the hospital, most of the cars were in the staff parking lot, but there were several parked near the emergency room. She knew the main entrance would be closed to visitors in the middle of the night, so she headed to where it looked like things were busy.

Before getting out of the car, Pacie looked around outside. Bright lights on poles reflected on the fog's water vapor, making it look as though something had been on fire and was now smoldering, spewing a thick smoke. The only person she saw outside was someone smoking a cigarette in the designated smoking area.

Pacie got out of the car and walked to the emergency entrance. A security guard saw her approaching and motioned for her to stand near the speaker on the hospital's brick wall.

"May I help you?" The guard's voice sounded robotic through the speaker.

"I'm Pacie Rose. I'm checking on my cousin, Irma Foster. Victor in the sleep study unit called me."

The guard nodded as if he knew all about it. "You can come in."

Pacie heard a buzz, then the emergency entrance double doors slid open. She walked inside, unsure how to get to the third floor from there. "How do I get to the sleep study unit?"

"Those elevators over there will get you where you need to go."

Pacie thanked him and walked toward the elevator, surprised there were so many serious situations that needed dealing with on a Monday night. There were lots of people and lots of beeping sounds in the somewhat chaotic atmosphere. Maybe this is why Irma could not be found, staff was busy attending to people who needed acute care.

Pacie was the only one in the elevator as she rode it up two floors. When she exited it and walked toward the unit, she saw someone walking down the hallway toward her. It was one of the techs.

When the tech was close enough for Pacie to talk to her without yelling, she said, "Kim, right?"

The woman looked at her intently, like a deer caught in headlights. "Oh, hi. You're Irma's friend."

"I'm Pacie, her cousin." Pacie knew the answer to the question before asking. "How's Irma? Did you find her?"

Kim began wringing her hands. "No, not yet. But I'm sure she can't be far. She probably found someplace good to sleep, without wires."

Pacie smiled. "Yeah."

"You can come with me to the unit," Kim said, walking past her.

Pacie followed her into the sleep study lab. She was not sure if she was supposed to be in there, but she wanted to see how things were set up.

"This is Pacie," Kim said to Victor who was sitting in

front of the monitors with an empty cup of coffee at his side. "Anything new with Irma?"

"Hi, Pacie," Victor said. "The guards are looking for her. Do you have a cellphone with you?"

Pacie reached into her satchel and pulled it out. "I do."

Victor verified her phone number. "I'll call you as soon as we find out anything."

"Sounds good." Pacie looked at the monitors and then out the window at the unit. "It looks like you both have a good view of the rooms. How did she escape?" Pacie smiled. She could tell both Kim and Victor felt awful about the situation.

Victor cleared his throat. "We're not sure. No alarms went off to alert us that she had been disconnected. Does she know how to operate this type of equipment?"

Pacie shrugged. "I don't think so."

"Holy crap," Victor said, looking less tense. "I know you. You're our local citizen reporter and the author of those Black Water mystery books, aren't you? It didn't connect with me at first when I heard your name."

"Irma and I have been known to do an investigation or two. Unofficial, of course."

"Of course," Victor said. "Do you have any idea where she would have gone?"

"I don't," Pacie said. "She came here to have a sleep study done because she's been sleepwalking and having bad dreams, but you already know all that. She would not intentionally just walk off the unit. She must be sleepwalking, just like you both expect."

"Thank you, anyway," Victor said.

"Is someone always watching the monitors?"

"Most of the time we both watch them," Victor said. "But when one of us goes on break, the other one watches all four. No one is ever gone that long."

The lab's phone rang. Kim answered it. "Sleep study lab. Kim speaking."

Pacie tried to hear the voice on the other end, but it was not loud enough.

"One guard, Sam, is on the fourth floor looking for her. I think Brian is up there, too."

Pacie glanced at Victor, who was looking back at the monitors and writing information on clipboards.

"Okay, then. Call me when you find her and I'll come to get her," Kim said.

When Kim hung up the telephone, Pacie said, "I take it they haven't found Irma yet?"

"No, not yet." Kim sat down next to Victor.

Kim and Victor appeared to be done talking. "I'll let you both get back to work. Is it okay if I go into her room?"

"Not a problem," Victor said. "You can wait there as long as you like."

Pacie thanked them and walked out of the lab. She walked into Irma's room; painfully aware she was being watched.

Irma, how did you turn off the alarm? Pacie turned on the room's light and walked over to the equipment. Electrodes, once attached to Irma's body, were still connected to cable clips. Irma must have ripped them off her body. But doing that would have set off alarms, so Irma must have silenced the machine.

The overbed vital sign monitor was still on, its blood pressure cuff dangled from the bed. Pacie could see on the screen that the alarm was on silence mode. It was possible that Irma could have done it herself, she was good at working with electronics. Once turned off, she could then disconnect herself and leave. But doing that would seem more like something a conscious person would do, not a sleepwalker.

There was also the problem of why the techs didn't see it happening, they were setting in front of the monitors watching the patients. One of them was probably on break, leaving the other to tend to other things like reconnecting a loose electrode in another patient's room. Could Irma have known when she was not being monitored and know that she could flee? Was it dumb luck? Or did she have help? But even that made no sense. Nothing made sense.

But no matter, what's done, is done. Irma needed to be found.

Pacie continued to look around the room for anything out of place and found nothing. The suspense novel Irma was reading lay on the bedside stand next to a pitcher of water. Her opened computer was sleeping on a small table. And the bathroom had a used toothbrush and paste.

Pacie glanced at the camera and decided she did not want to set in a chair being watched until they found Irma, so she walked out of Room Four to the unit's waiting area. But there was nothing she could do there aside from sleep and wake up with a stiff neck.

Then it occurred to her that Kim was walking from the far end of the hallway when she first saw her. She must have come from the exit door at the end. And Kim told whoever she was talking to on the phone that security was on the fourth floor. They must think Irma had gone up there.

Fourth floor, here I come.

Pacie left the sleep study unit and walked into the long corridor. The door at the end of the hallway was an emergency exit and would certainly be unlocked. Whether she could get on the fourth floor was yet to be seen.

Doubting Irma would go into any of the rooms along the hallway; she tested them anyway. They were all locked and probably already searched by the staff. When she reached the exit door, she opened it and walked onto the landing. She looked up and down the concrete steps. Seeing no one, she climbed the stairs to the fourth floor. The stairs went up one more level after that, but it looked to be where maintenance would go.

Ah, yes. The psych floor. I think this was closed down a while back.

She could see flickering lights through the door's window. The guards were probably still searching for Irma.

When Pacie opened the door, she could hear people talking at the end of the long dark corridor. The lighting was poor, but she could tell that there were two people down there, probably the guards, and it sounded like they were talking to someone. Was it Irma? Were they trying to persuade her to return to her room?

Pacie reached into her satchel and pulled out a small flashlight and began walking toward them. She was halfway there when there was a loud crash, prompting the two men to run back down the corridor toward her.

"You don't belong on this floor," one guard yelled as he ran past Pacie. "Leave, now."

"Don't go down there. Come with us," the other guard said, his voice pitched with fear. He slowed enough to tug on Pacie's arm, trying to get her to turn around. When Pacie stopped moving, the guard released her and sped off.

Shocked by the guards' reaction, she stood there, watching them run away. Was Irma threatening their lives?

"Did you find Irma?" Pacie shouted at them. But the men were through the door before she heard an answer. Now she was alone, except for whatever was at the end of the hallway.

Then it came back to her; she remembered the reason the lockdown unit had stopped being used. Apparently, as the rumor goes, there was a man who was admitted as a psych patient who belonged to a satanic cult. A short while later, strange things began happening. It started with items being moved or they would simply come up missing. But this guy kept chanting in a language no one knew, and they said it was true, he summoned the devil. When a woman was found hanging from the neck in a safe room, and minor demons began showing themselves to patients and staff, people just ran off the unit. A priest was even called out to bless the floor, but it must not have worked.

From what Pacie saw so far, people had certainly left in a hurry and never went back.

Pacie could not be more creeped out. Her gut was telling her to run out of the place like the guards, but if Irma was being harmed, she could not and would not leave.

She shined her light toward whatever was down there, hiding in the shadows. Pacie could see the slightest of movement but could not make out who it was.

"Irma, is that you?" Pacie stood in place, waiting for an answer.

Pacie crept forward a few feet and stopped. In the black, nearly opaque light at the end of the hallway she saw a wheelchair lying on its side and a shape ever slightly moving in a corner of blackness. Was someone holding Irma hostage? But if it was Irma, why wasn't she answering?

When Pacie moved forward a few more feet, she saw what appeared to be someone lying on the floor next to the wheelchair. Had someone done something to Irma?

Without thinking, Pacie ran to it and to whatever was shrouded in darkness. She pulled the wheelchair away just as her flashlight died and knelt next to the body. Even though everything was cast in deep shadow, Pacie knew this was not Irma. But no matter who it was, they needed help. She gently shook the shoulder and said, "Are you alright?"

Pacie let go of the gelid shoulder, keenly aware that the person before her was a corpse.

Then a sharp snapping sound caused her to look toward the darkest corner where the stench of rotting flesh was emanating. She was only a few feet away from whatever was there. Despite that, she could not see what occupied the space.

When the body on the floor before Pacie spasmed, she was so startled that she fell backward onto her bottom. The floor was icy and covered with grit. Now she understood why the guards had decided to neglect their duty of securing the floor and sped out of there like fraidy-cats. But she had to ask again. She had to be sure. Her voice quivered. "Irma?"

A gravelly voice like that from a nightmare said, "No. But you will do just fine."

Pacie twisted around so fast to a sprinter's position—as if her feet were in starting blocks—her shoes slipped on the debris, which acted like small ball bearings below her. Her right knee smacked the tiled floor. She winced momentarily but was able to get her footing and race down the hallway toward the exit. But before she reached it, she heard Irma's voice, weak and almost unidentifiable.

"Pacie?"

Slowing to a jog, and close to opening the exit door, Pacie turned and looked back down the hallway from where she had come. Irma was standing in the corridor, near the double doors. She saw the things emerging from the shadows.

"Irma, run!" Pacie ran back to Irma, pausing only a moment to see what was coming after them. In her mind what she saw registered as a walking dead patient and a tall, skinny guy like an undertaker. Slenderman was real.

Chapter 19

PACIE WAS STILL PULLING on Irma when they reached the sleep study unit. Having taken no time to call anyone, it surprised Kim and Victor when they burst through the door and stood in the hallway between the rooms, gasping for air.

"Kim, call security," Victor said as he ran out of the lab and up to Irma. "Are you alright?"

Irma grumbled.

"Let's get you back in bed," Victor said, guiding Irma to her room.

"I might be a senior citizen, but I'm not crippled," Irma said, resisting the hold he had on her arm.

Pacie followed them into the room.

"I called Sam, he's on his way," Kim said, rushing in behind Pacie.

Pacie stood next to the bed while Irma pulled up the covers and closed her eyes. She looked at Irma, and then at Victor. "What time do we have to be out of here this morning? I think she's going back to sleep."

"Sleeping is fine," Victor said. "The doctor usually comes

in between seven and nine. After that, you're free to go."

Victor and Kim began reconnecting Irma to the wired monitors. Pacie watched until they finished assessing her, then said, "Can I talk with you both?"

"Come with us back to the lab," Victor said. "We'll talk there."

Pacie looked at Irma, tucked snuggly in bed, then followed the techs into the laboratory.

"Have a seat," Victor said, pulling a chair out from under a counter.

Pacie sat down as Kim turned her attention to the monitors. Then a security guard walked into the unit. He looked in Irma's room and then came into the lab.

"I see the patient is back. Is she alright?"

"She is, and she's fine, Sam," Victor said, turning his chair to face Pacie and the guard at the door.

The guard looked at Pacie. "You were up on the fourth floor. Is that where she was?"

Pacie watched him cross his arms to steady a rather pronounced tremor. "Yeah, she was."

Victor leaned forward. "So, what exactly happened?"

Pacie cleared her throat, still tight and dry from the stress. Pacie explained Irma was standing in the hallway when she found her, not seeming to know what was going on. That she must have sleepwalked up there. Then she looked at the guard. "Who were those other people? You saw them, didn't you? I heard you talking to them."

"People?" Victor said, surprised. "There are no people on the fourth floor. And I'm amazed Irma could get up there because that door is always locked."

"Someone must've left it unlocked," Pacie said. She looked at the guard who was still staring at her. "Those people, who were they?"

Sam shook his head. "I don't know. I mean, I have a hunch that they're the reason the floor was closed in the first place. One of them, anyway. The tall one is new."

"So you check that floor?" Pacie asked.

"Unfortunately, we do. Not often, but it is part of our patrol."

"You said the tall one was new. What do you mean?" Pacie rubbed her aching knee.

"On the night shift, Brian and I are the lucky ones who have to go up there. Rarely, we see something that looks like a patient in the shadows. He's the one that's supposed to be the satanic worshipper that was a patient there a long time ago." Sam brought his hands to his face as if he wanted to hide. "But that skinny, faceless one is new. I first saw it last week. Brian saw it too."

"Were you talking to it? I heard people talking. What did it say?"

"Oh, man," Sam said, fidgeting. "It told me and Brian to leave. It said we were next—to die."

Victor's chair creaked when he leaned back and clasped his hands behind his head as if enjoying a rather humorous campfire story. "No way, that's just a rumor. They're real people and someone needs to go up there and get them out."

"Have you been on the fourth floor?" Pacie asked Victor.

"No, it's condemned because of asbestos, lead pipes,

something like that. Ya need a respirator and hazmat suit to go up there."

Sam shook his head. "That's what they tell people to keep them off the floor. Brian and I don't have to put that stuff on."

Pacie believed what the guard was saying because she knew what she saw, and they were not people who happened to wander up there, as Irma had. She looked at Victor. "I hate to say it but I agree with Sam. What I saw was the reason that floor is closed."

Victor laughed, and Sam was no less anxious.

"You guys," Kim said, sounding annoyed. "Irma is our focus here. Remember? From what I've heard so far, she was sleepwalking, and our elite security guards could not find her. It took Irma's friend to do the hard work."

"Her cousin," Pacie corrected. "But I'm still unsure how she was able to walk off the unit."

"I had to unsilence the main monitor," Kim said. "Irma must've been watching me set it up and then unconsciously, because she was sleepwalking, turned it off."

"Or those things upstairs turned it off for her," Sam said, walking swiftly out of the lab.

"I guess he didn't want any follow-up on that comment," Victor said, amused.

Pacie looked up at the ceiling, wondering where it met the floor above. She could not tell, but it unnerved her that only a few feet separated the floors.

"Do you have any more questions for me?"

"No," Victor said. "Sounds like it's been a rather eventful night for you. Are you going to wait in Irma's room?"

The clock on the wall read four-fifteen. "Yeah, I'll stay with her."

"There's a blanket and pillow in the closet if you need it," Kim said, flipping the pen in her hand back and forth.

"Thanks," Pacie said, standing. She cringed in pain from having slammed her knee on the floor earlier.

"Are you okay?" Kim asked, watching Pacie touch her knee.

"I'm fine. I just hurt my knee on the fourth floor."

"You should file an incident report with the office," Victor said.

Pacie nodded and babied her knee as she walked out of the lab. Irma was lying in the same position as when Pacie had left her. She looked at the monitor displaying the vital signs; everything was normal. Pacie wondered if Irma would even remember the events of the night.

Pacie took the pillow and blanket from the closet and sat in the cushioned chair next to the window. Outside, the ever-present fog hovered over the parking lot. She positioned the flat pillow under her head and closed her eyes. Sleep would not come easy.

After fidgeting in the chair for a while, she finally gave up. She remembered seeing a coffee machine in the main lobby. Irma was snoring; Pacie was sure the techs would watch Irma's every move for the rest of the night.

With her satchel crossbody, Pacie left the room and walked to the lab. "I can't sleep, so I'm going to get a cup of coffee."

"Sure thing," Victor said with a nod.

Pacie walked to the elevator, half debating whether to go back up to the fourth floor. But since Irma was safe, there was no reason to do that. Unless, of course, her investigative nature wanted her to record the haunting, but now was not the time.

She got in the empty elevator and took it down to the main lobby. The vending machines were across the large open space next to the closed gift shop and café.

The hospital decorators had placed tall, large-leaved plants around a bubbling water fountain in its center. Pacie smiled as she approached the ferns and palms and walked up to the spraying water, but something was not right. Then it occurred to her; it was the air. Instead of a fresh, earthy aroma, there was a slight odor. Pacie had smelled it a few times in the last week, and she associated it with whatever was going on in Black Water.

There was no doubt that one of the entities, the one that looked like Slenderman, on the fourth floor was causing the child abductions and murder. Now it surely had its sights on Irma. At least Irma was fine, as far as she could tell. Sure, she could confront this evil thing upstairs, but Pacie did not know how to stop it. Though she remembered reading that it took goodness and prayers to drive it away. And that the person who conjured it had to stop thinking about it. They had called a priest out to bless the floor years ago—he might need to come back.

The sound of falling water diminished as Pacie approached the coffee machine. Fortunately, it took a card, and she did not have to scrounge around her purse for quarters. She punched the code for black coffee and watched the cup, somewhat tilted, fall down the chute. A black stream of coffee trickled into the cup.

Pacie brought the liquid stimulant—at least she hoped—to her lips, expecting it to be scalding hot, but instead it was lukewarm.

The rattle of metal made Pacie jump. An early attendant was placing fresh cookies and brownies in the cafe's showcase. She walked over to it and looked through the glass.

"What time do you open?" Pacie asked, hoping to get a dose of sugar to go with the caffeine.

"Not until six," she said. Her plastic gloves had hints of what had to be chocolate frosting on the fingertips.

"I'll come back. Thank you."

Pacie strolled around the lobby, sipping her coffee. The dimmed lights caused shadows in the corners. She felt like she was being watched, but she was not fully recovered from what she experienced on the old psych unit. She expected to see movement among the shadows and supernatural beings stagger out of the gloom.

A couple of employees, nurses she presumed, walked inside through the main sliding doors and toward the elevator. A security guard, who she had not noticed earlier, stood at the front entrance. He looked like the other guard that was with Sam on the fourth floor. She hoped he would let her ask him a few questions.

When Pacie got closer, she recognized him. He was the guard that held her arm for a moment, trying to stop her from getting any closer to what lay at the end of the hallway.

As she approached, Pacie could tell he recognized her. His identification badge had the name Brian printed on it.

"Hi. Are you the guard that was looking for my cousin

Irma?" Pacie could not help but notice that he looked as frightened as Sam had been.

He nodded. "I'm surprised you're still here. I would've left this place a long time ago."

"If my cousin wasn't here, I would've." Pacie sipped her coffee. "Sam said you guys have to go up there every once in a while and check the place out. That wouldn't be my ideal job."

Brian was not comfortable with the conversation. "We go together, do what we have to do, and then leave."

Pacie nodded. "Yeah, that's not a place to hang out in."

Brian nodded at a worker coming into the hospital.

"Do you keep the door to the fourth floor locked?" Pacie was trying to figure out how Irma got up there in the first place.

"Always. All the doors to the floor are locked, even the elevator door won't open onto it. That's one thing we check when we have to go up there."

"What have you seen up there?" Pacie could tell he did not want to answer the question. "I'm asking because I want to compare it to what I saw."

Brian put his hands on his hips and shook his head. "Most of the time we don't see anything, it's just a feeling we get when we're up there. A bad feeling, like something evil is watching us. We hear noises mostly. Noises like a door being closed—of course, there's no breeze up there—and when we check it out, we find nothing. But on rare occasions, I see him, the satanic patient. And there are little demons, that's what I call them, running around. Those things don't happen very often; but when they do, I say I'm going to quit and find a job that doesn't have that shit to deal with. The only reason I haven't walked off the job already is that the rest of what I have to do is gravy and the pay isn't bad."

"What about the tall thing? How often have you seen that?"

Brian shook his head. "It's new. And I get the feeling it's worse than the devil-worshiping guy. I've only seen it in the last week."

At least Brian's story matched with Sam's. "Have you told the hospital? Maybe they can send a priest up there again or something."

"We have, but it doesn't do any good. Either they think we're exaggerating, or they don't want to deal with it. Either way, nothing gets done. They still send us up there. I suppose that since no one has been hurt, they're just going to live with it. Or rather, *we* have to live with it. I think it would take someone dying before they gave a crap."

Pacie knew what he was talking about. People would rather ignore paranormal activity than deal with it and hope it went away on its own.

"Did the tall, skinny one ever say anything to you?" Pacie sipped her nearly cold coffee.

Brian thought for a moment. "It told us to get out and that we were going to die."

"Did it ever give itself a name?"

"No. I don't want to know its name; I want it to leave."

"Thank you, Brian. I'm going back up to the sleep unit and see how Irma's doing."

"I wouldn't go back up on the fourth floor anymore if I were you."

"The door should be locked. I don't think Irma, or I could

get up there even if we wanted to."

Pacie walked slowly away, thinking. So what did she know so far? The tall entity was probably Slenderman. But why was it here in the hospital? Was it because Irma was here? Is it after her? If so, for what reason?

The main thing though, even if Pacie could never answer the questions, was how to get rid of it. The ghost of that patient hasn't harmed the guards, but Slenderman could. He has already taken children and caused a murder. Irma was probably sleepwalking because of him. So the question is, how to get rid of it. Speaking with Father Murphy was the only answer.

Pacie moseyed around a little more to pass the time. The hospital was waking up and Dr. Plum would be there soon.

She threw away her empty cup and took the stairs to the third floor; the exercise would help keep her awake. Pacie listened for sounds as she ascended the steps. She wanted to hear if anyone was going onto the fourth floor, but no one was.

When Pacie reached the third floor, part of her wanted to continue up to the lockdown unit and see if the door was locked. She looked at her watch; it was near six o'clock. She had time to check it out. Pacie stood there debating with herself. It wouldn't hurt to just test the door and see if it would open. If it allowed her to enter, she would tell Victor or Kim to call security and have them lock it. Her testing the door would be a safety measure and a good idea. She was too good at convincing herself to do things that would be better off left to someone else.

Pacie continued climbing the stairs to the fourth floor. Her knee ached, but it was not going to stop her. It was dark past the window; the guards had turned off the lights. She rested a hand on the handle and after a few seconds of debate, pulled. The door opened.

Oh my god. Now I have to investigate.

Chapter 20

PACIE PULLED THE DOOR open. A puff of stale air blew into her face. She stepped inside, letting the door close behind her. It was quiet; she knew she was alone. She reached into her satchel and took out her flashlight, then remembered it had died on her the last time she was up there. She turned it on and off a couple of times. It had not miraculously fixed itself, so she dropped it back inside her bag.

It was dark, but the few emergency lights that glowed along the floor gave enough illumination for her to keep going. Pacie walked into the nurses' station and looked around. She picked up one of several papers that were scattered on the desk. It was too dark to read them, but she could make out that one was a sign-in sheet and some others were a doctor's progress notes that had fallen from an open and unclamped chart.

Pacie did not plan to stay on the floor. She did not want to miss Dr. Plum, but she wanted to get a better feel for the abandoned unit.

She walked to the open double doors and the area where Irma was standing. Where had she come from? One of the rooms? The first room on the right was a waiting area or a place for visitors to talk with patients. Maybe Irma had been in there. The blinds on the windows were partly open, letting some of the early morning dawn brighten the area, but it was still too dark to see well.

The room on the other side of the hall was a small kitchen with an ice machine, refrigerator, and a sink. Again, maybe Irma had been in there.

But what Pacie really wanted to see was the end of the hall where the entities were. She did not get the feeling they were still there. There were no unusual sounds, and the shadows at the end of the hall were not as opaque. She could see objects like equipment that had been pushed into it. She could see the red exit sign that she did not remember seeing earlier.

With measured steps, Pacie began walking down the long corridor, doing her best to avoid the stretchers, a standing scale, and other utilitarian objects that cluttered it. Muted light from rooms was spilling into the hallway from the rising sun.

Pacie kept going until she stood several feet from the end of the hallway where she had seen Slenderman. He was not there. Aside from a wheelchair on its side and several walkers, there was nothing alive, or rather, nothing moving.

A small object, like a pen, lay on the floor. A weak beam of light was coming out its end. She picked up the flashlight, wondering who it belonged to and why was it dropped. She knew perfectly well why someone dropped it. They were frightened by the monsters they met at the end of the hall-way and while in a panic, dropped it as they were fleeing. She held it up to the light coming in from the exit door's window.

Black Water General was stamped on its barrel.

Pacie shined the weak light along the floor, looking for anything that would seem like a clue. There was nothing, only a few scuff marks on the floor.

The stench she had smelled earlier was not there. The creatures were gone. Had they gone to other parts of the hospital or somewhere else?

The sound of ambulance and police sirens caught Pacie's attention as she looked at her watch. She had better get back to Irma, just in case the doctor visited early.

Pacie moved a walker and tried to open the exit door, but it would not open. She turned off the useless penlight and put it in her pocket as she walked back down the corridor, past the nurses' station. Whatever had been on this floor earlier was not there now. Maybe the entity was where the ambulance was headed, having already wreaked havoc at the new location.

When Pacie reached Irma's room, she was dressed and eating breakfast at the small table by the window.

"Where have you been?" Irma asked, stuffing scrambled eggs into her mouth.

"Just walking around, trying to stay awake."

Irma sipped her coffee, then said, "I slept better than I thought I would. I haven't slept through the night in a long time."

Pacie was not entirely surprised; she was more disappointed. "You mean you don't remember?"

"Remember what?"

Kim and Dr. Plum walked into the room.

"Hi, Irma. How are you feeling this morning?" Dr. Plum

asked. A white lab coat covered his podgy build, and a stethoscope hung around his neck folds.

Irma picked up the paper napkin beside her plate and wiped her mouth. "Hi, Doctor. I feel fine."

Doctor Plum adjusted his glasses. "Do you remember anything that happened during the night?'

Irma thought a moment. "Not really. I had a bad dream. I was looking for Mr. Dibble, my dog, and I couldn't find him. I looked all over the hospital for him. I heard him barking." Irma paused, then said, "I don't remember the rest."

The penlight was about to fall out of Pacie's pocket, so she sat it on the table. She heard Kim gasp.

"You've been having bouts of sleepwalking. Do you remember those?"

"Only if I wake up or I see something unusual like dirt on my feet when I get out of bed in the morning."

"Do you remember sleepwalking last night?" Dr. Plum asked.

"What? I sleepwalked last night?" Irma put a hand over her heart. "You're not going to admit me to the hospital, are you?"

Doctor Plum smiled. "No. What I want to start with though, are lifestyle and self-care habits. No caffeine or alcohol before bed. And things like practicing relaxation techniques might help. Also, I want you to keep a sleep journal and to see a counselor who will help you with these things."

"What if all that doesn't work?" Irma asked.

"Then we'll have to look at medication like Valium. I'll also refer you to a somnologist or neurologist for further evaluation." Dr. Plum turned toward the door. "And don't forget to schedule an appointment with my office and we'll see how things are going."

Irma pushed her plate away. "I will."

Doctor Plum spoke with Kim for a moment, then they both went into another patient's room.

"I suppose as soon as you get your discharge instructions, you're free to go," Pacie said, watching Irma stare off into space. "I want you to stay with me for a while longer."

"I'll be fine at my place," Irma said halfheartedly.

"Just until this all goes away." Pacie knew Irma was worried about another knife incident. And so was she.

Irma leaned toward Pacie and whispered. "I know what's causing this."

Pacie looked at Irma, who was as serious as a heart attack. She knew what her cousin was about to say.

"It's Slenderman."

Pacie nodded. "I was thinking that, too."

"But I don't want to say that to the doctor, he'll think I'm crazy."

"I know. We need to get rid of that thing." Pacie was divided in thought. She wanted Irma to get the treatment she needed, but she also knew that if they mentioned Irma taking a knife into Pacie's room while sleepwalking, they would probably admit her, and who knew where things would go from there. But Irma was not crazy, it was Slenderman that was affecting her. Even that thought was crazy. Maybe she herself needed to be admitted to the psych unit. At least it would be the new unit and not the fourth floor.

Irma stood up and walked to her suitcase. "I don't know

how to get rid of it; get it out of my head."

"I don't either, not really. I'll talk to Father Murphy and see what he says."

"What about going back to the mansion in the woods?"

Pacie blew out a puff of air. "After I speak with Father, I guess we can go to the mansion and look for Slenderman."

"What did you say?" Kim was standing in the room with a clipboard of papers.

"Nothing," Pacie said, leaning back in her chair.

Kim walked up to the table. "Where did you get that penlight?"

Pacie picked it up and that's when she noticed it had the initials K. C. on it. "Is this yours?"

Kim took the penlight that Pacie handed her. "Yes, it is."

"So you were on the fourth floor, too. Did you see anything?"

Kim held the clipboard close to her chest. "I don't know, did you?"

Pacie nodded. "I did. What did you see?"

"I, I saw an animated corpse and a guy dressed in black that was tall and skinny and ... evil. I was so scared that I dropped my penlight."

Pacie was relieved. Here was a nonbiased, logical person who saw the same thing she had seen. It even verified what the guard had told her. "That's what I saw."

Kim stared at Pacie, then said, "Let's get this paperwork done and I'll let you both get out of here."

With the discharge instructions in hand, Irma and Pacie walked off the unit and out of the hospital. All Pacie had to do was to figure out how to get rid of Slenderman. She knew it would not be easy. She did not even know where to start, but the town's priest was a step in the right direction. At least she hoped.

Chapter 21

WHEN PACIE OPENED HER front door, Mr. Dibble bolted
out, almost knocking over both her and Irma. "He was in a
hurry. Guess I can't blame him."

Irma sat the suitcase on the floor just inside the door. She
looked back at Mr. Dibble, who was kicking up pieces of grass
clippings with his hind paws. "He can stay out there a bit."

"I don't know about you," Pacie said, walking toward the
dining room, "but I'm starved."

"I've already eaten a little bit of breakfast. That is, until
I found out I sleepwalked again and lost my appetite," Irma
said as she followed Pacie through the connecting rooms to
the kitchen. "What are you making?"

"Have a seat at the kitchen table and I'll whip up some
scrambled eggs and sausage patties. Oh, and Mr. Dibble's food
is still in that cabinet over there."

Irma filled the dog dishes with water and kibble and then
sat back down. "I've been thinking." She plopped her elbows
on the table. "I think you should lock me inside my room
tonight. This house has a skeleton key for that, doesn't it?"

"Ah, yeah. I just have to find it." Pacie put the sausage patties into the hot frying pan, causing an immediate sizzle. "I guess I could do that. I just have to find the key. But what if you have to use the bathroom during the night? How are you going to do that? Ring the old servants call bell?"

Irma leaned back in her chair so that Pacie could put the plates, silverware, and hot coffee on the table. "I got it. I'll call you on my cellphone. If I can do that, then you'll know I'm awake and won't — hurt you."

Pacie walked back to the counter and whisked the eggs. "Okay. That makes sense. But it makes me feel like you're a werewolf and I have to lock you up because the full moon is coming."

"Is there a full moon tonight?" Irma nervously turned the coffee-filled cup that Pacie had sat in front of her so that she could pick it up by the handle.

Pacie sipped her coffee. "I don't know. It's sometime soon. Tonight or tomorrow maybe."

Irma stood up with a groan. "I hear Mr. Dibble. I'm going to let him in."

Pacie nodded and watched Irma leave the room. Locking her in the bedroom and using a cellphone for communication sounded like a good idea, but how long could something like that go on? They had to get rid of Slenderman, if that really was what was causing Irma's sleepwalking, and get their lives back to normal.

Pacie had just finished plating the scrambled eggs and sausage when her cellphone rang. She took it from her pocket. "Hi, Char. What's up?"

"Nothing. I was just wondering how Irma was doing. Mom said she was in the hospital for sleepwalking."

"Irma's fine. She had a sleep study test done last night." Pacie did not want to worry her granddaughter. "She's going to stay with me for a while—her and Mr. Dibble. They're outside right now."

"That's good. I was worried about her. I'll let mom know."

"So what are you going to be up to this week?"

"I have to babysit tonight for the Anderson's."

"On a Tuesday night? What's going on?"

"It's their anniversary. Fourteen years."

"That's nice," Pacie said. "They have two kids, don't they?"

"Yeah, six and nine, or something like that. They can be a little bratty, though."

Pacie laughed. "At least it'll give you some money to put towards a car of your own so that you don't have to keep driving your mom and dad's."

Charlotte sighed. "At this rate, it'll take years."

"I'll keep an eye out for a good deal."

"Thanks, Grandma."

Thoughts of the abductions entered Pacie's mind. "I know you know this, but because of what's been happening around town, lock the doors and close the curtains. And don't let anyone into the house or talk to any strangers."

"I'll lock things up. But I'll be fine, I know the neighbors."

"I know. Call me if you need anything. I'll be by the phone."

"Okay," Charlotte said. "I gotta go; the oven timer just went off. Tell Irma I said hi.

After they said their goodbyes, Pacie walked into the study

and plugged in her cellphone, laying it on her desk beside the laptop. She would eat breakfast, get a shower, and then head out to speak with Father Murphy. And it probably would not hurt to meet with Professor Edward Beasley, Black Water College's lead anthropology and archeology professor.

Pacie picked up the phone, swiped through the contacts, and dialed the professor's office.

"Black Water College, Professor Beasley's office. May I help you?"

"Hi, this is Pacie Rose I—"

"Oh, hi, Pacie. How's it going? Another new case? I'm sure it's about the strange goings-on in town. Am I right?"

"You got it. How are you, Aileen? Is the professor keeping you busy researching any new acquisitions?"

"Of course," Aileen said, snapping her gum. "Just this morning he told me about the head of a cat from the Late Period and Ptolemaic Period in Egypt. He wants me to do a little preliminary research on it."

"Sounds interesting. I wish I had your job."

"No you don't. I end up taking my work home, which isn't always that bad. But the professor lives and breathes archeology and expects me to do the same." Aileen laughed. "I'm exaggerating—a little. Were you wanting to speak with him?"

"I'd like to meet him today. Does he have any free time?"

"He does, but let me double-check," Aileen said, clicking the keyboard. "He's free today after his morning lecture. So stop in between eleven and one o'clock. Does that work for you?"

"It does. I'm going to meet with Father Murphy first, then

Irma and I will be there."

"Okay, see you both then."

Irma and Mr. Dibble came back into the house, clearly making their presence known. Irma was telling Mr. Dibble not to run while he ran to the kitchen while Mr. Dibble ignored her and hotfooted it to his doggie bowls.

"So what are our plans today?" Irma said, following Pacie from the study and into the kitchen. They sat across from each other at the table and looked at the food.

"Let's see Father first thing then this morning and then make our way over to the college to see Professor Beasley."

"That sounds good," Irma said, biting into the nearly cold sausage. "What about the mansion? I think you should go back there—with me this time."

Pacie was not fond of going back to the mansion, especially since she was sure she saw someone watching her. But she got the feeling that—somehow—Slenderman had something to do with the place.

"Did you hear me?" Irma said, rapping her fork on her plate.

"Yes, but I don't know if we'll have time to do it today. By the time we finish with Father and the professor, it will be too late to go out there. I would prefer to leave first thing in the morning."

"Tomorrow morning?"

"Yeah. We'll leave early."

Irma sipped her coffee. "I'm both looking forward to it and reluctant to go out there at the same time."

Pacie nodded. "I'm just reluctant."

Chapter 22

IRMA PUT MR. DIBBLE in the backseat of Pacie's SUV and then climbed in the passenger seat, placing her backpack in the footwell. "I'm ready."

"I hope we get some answers," Pacie said, driving down the driveway. The lingering fog cast somber shapes and shadows over the landscape. "We're running out of time. We have to stop the monster before there's another child abducted or someone else is murdered."

"I don't believe it," Irma said, looking at her cellphone. "There was another murder this morning while I was still at the sleep study."

"This morning?" Pacie remembered hearing sirens when she was on the fourth floor, looking around for the second time. "What happened?"

"Says here that an elderly woman was strangled to death while she slept in her bed. The neighbor girl is suspected of committing the crime. There aren't any details."

"Maybe we should talk to Haley or Chief Malone and see if we can find out more."

"You mean like Slenderman telling the girl to do it so that she could get a reward and live in his palace?"

"Exactly."

"I'll text Haley. I don't think Chief Malone likes us much. He thinks we meddle in the investigations."

"We do." Pacie laughed.

Pacie pulled up to Sacred Heart Catholic Church. Morning Mass was over. Irma left her backpack in the car. They walked up the stone steps and went through the large double doors. Inside the vestibule, the second set of doors was open. A few people sat in the pews, praying.

"I don't see him," Irma whispered.

"He's probably in the sacristy or maybe in the rectory."

They dipped their fingers in the holy water font and blessed themselves before entering the body of the church. Pacie motioned for Irma to walk around the back of the church, behind the pews. When they reached the altar rail they stopped. Past the sanctuary, the door to the sacristy was open. Pacie could see the young Father Murphy standing at the sacrarium, the sink that drains directly into the earth.

"He's busy," Irma said quietly.

Father Murphy looked up, dried his hands, and walked to the door. "Well, hello, Pacie and Irma. Good to see you both. Is there something I can help you with?"

"Father, I'm sure you're aware of all the strange things that have been happening lately—kidnapping and murders—so we wanted to ask you a few questions."

"Of course." Father Murphy closed the sacristy door and walked past the alter. "I am indeed aware of all the evil and chaos that has been happening. Let's talk in my office."

They walked with Father to the rectory next door. His office was the first room on the left.

"Please, have a seat," Father said as he sat behind his desk. "How can I help you?"

"This sounds weird, but have you heard of Slenderman?" Pacie asked.

"Why am I not surprised you mention such a thing as Slenderman," Father Murphy said. "I don't know all the details of what's been happening in town, but it's my understanding that Slenderman is a made-up character. But this entity, if one were to call it that, has been around for ages. For example, do you remember hearing of the Pied Piper?"

"I do," Irma said. "It's a fairy tale. Didn't he drive the rats out of some town in Germany?"

"That's partly true. Throughout history, there have been demons who want to destroy humans, send us to Hell. In this instance, in the Middle Ages, a ratcatcher was called to the German town of Hamelin. It's said that this colorfully clothed piper could lure rats away with his magic pipe. This pied piper did what he was asked to do but when the rats were gone, the citizens refused to pay him for his service as they had promised. The Pied Piper retaliated by using his magical powers to lead the children away; never to be seen again. This Slenderman, as you call him, could be another one of Satan's demons unleashed upon the Earth."

"If that is true," Pacie said, "what has Black Water done to summon such madness?"

"I don't know," Father said, "but I don't think Satan needs

a reason to set evil upon the world."

"The big question is," Irma said, "is how do we get rid of it?"

Father glanced up at the painting of the Sacred Heart of Jesus on the wall near his desk—with its flaming heart of thorns. "To combat evil, it takes righteousness and purity."

"But where do we find such goodness that will send Slenderman packing?" Pacie asked.

"You, Pacie." He smiled and looked at Irma. "You both."

"I hate to tell you, Father, but I'm not exactly a saint," Pacie said.

"We can fix that."

"You can?"

"We can." Father opened a desk drawer and took out a necklace with a three-inch crucifix attached. He handed it to Pacie. "This crucifix is blessed. Wear it always."

"I'm not questioning your knowledge in such things," Pacie said, "but I think it'll take more than a crucifix to get rid of this entity."

"You're right. A crucifix won't make you pure of soul, but the Sacrament of Reconciliation will. Meet me at the confessional box." Father stood and began walking toward the door. He stopped and turned around. "Immediately."

Pacie looked at Irma as she put the crucifix around her neck. "I guess he means both of us."

"I wasn't planning on this," Irma said with a huff.

"Neither was I, but I'm sure we're due for it, anyway. And if it helps to get rid of Slenderman, we should be running to the confessional."

"You, maybe," Irma said.

After their confessions, they walked back out to the car.

"Now we can't do anything to ruin this," Pacie said, climbing into the driver's seat.

"Like what? I don't do anything that bad in the first place."

"I know, but we have to play it safe. So don't swear."

"That's a sin?"

"I don't know, but I don't want to take any chances."

"Smoking isn't a sin, is it?" Irma said, taking a cigarette from her fanny pack.

"I don't think so. It'll just send you to an early grave."

Irma cracked her window, thought a moment, then placed the cigarette back into its pack. "Professor Beasley next?"

"Yep."

When they reached the college, Pacie parked near the grass so that Mr. Dibble could get out for a moment. When he finished his task and was back in the car, they walked inside Black Water College. Students, young and old, were rushing around as if they were going to be late for class.

Professor Beasley's office was on the first floor, down a corridor where other teachers had their offices. His was at the end of the long hallway.

The door was open, so they walked inside and up to Aileen's desk.

"Hello, Pacie and Irma," Aileen said, smiling as she put a hand on top of a stack of books next to her. "This is some of the research I'm working on. The Ptolemaic Period in Egypt is quite interesting. It's when the capital Alexandria was completed and the ancient Library of Alexandria drew in scholars. But it all came to an end in 31 BC when the Romans defeated them. And Cleopatra committed suicide."

"Sounds interesting," Pacie said. "Is the professor planning a trip to Egypt?"

"He is, but I don't know when. There have been several discoveries there that he wants to assess."

"Are you going with him?"

"I'm not sure. It depends on the college's budget. You know how everything comes down to money."

"I know. But it would be fun."

"No arguments here," Aileen said, lifting the phone's receiver. "I know you're probably in a hurry. I'll buzz him just to make sure he's not in the middle of anything."

After a moment, the professor's office door opened. "Well, come on in you two. Have a seat. How can I help you?"

"Thank you," Pacie said as she and Irma each sat in upholstered wing-back chairs, while the professor sat on the leather couch. It was as though he had brought furnishings from his home to decorate his office.

Pacie liked Professor Beasley. He reminded her of the typical absent-minded professor with a disheveled suit and tie that hung off a scrawny body. His dark-rimmed glasses had thick lenses, and he was, of course, forgetful. Yet the clumsy professor was always willing to help Pacie.

"I'll bet you're here doing research for your latest book," the professor said. "I'll help you any way I can."

"Thank you, Professor, but we're trying to figure out how to find and capture the monster who's been abducting kids and committing murders around town."

"One person doing all that?" The professor cupped his chin.

"We believe so," Pacie said. "This maniac is persuasive and able to convince people, typically young people, to do whatever he says."

"What a scoundrel," the professor said. "I really should pay more attention to the news, but I've been in the process of acquiring a cat-like head sculpture of the deity Bastet."

"She's a goddess of protection, isn't she?" Irma said, leaning forward.

"Very good, Irma. You are correct. She's also the protector of cats, fertility, and other things."

Pacie rubbed the back of her tense neck. "Professor, do you remember a mansion in the woods that I think was built by Captain Perry a long time ago?"

"I do indeed." The professor stood and went to one of his many bookcases. His office was full of shelves and books, like a mini-library. He removed a hardback, blew dust from its brown cover, and sat back down. He thumbed through the pages. "Captain Perry became wealthy shipping lumber during the peak of the lumber industry, around eighteen-ninety, typically white and red pine, by using schooners to sail to places like Chicago. Later, he built a mansion for his pregnant wife around eighteen-ninety-five. Sad thing is, she died in childbirth and so did the baby. He lived there alone for the rest of his life. When he would sail out, the mansion sat alone and when he came back, he was little motivated to do any upkeep. After his death in eighteen-ninety-six, it fell into disrepair. Later, the state bought land in that area, selling some of it to Bulwark's for the nuclear power plant. They tore down the old captain's home. At least I think so, this book doesn't say for sure. Anyway, if they didn't demolish it, it must be nothing more than a pile of rubble, overtaken by the forest vegetation. Why do you ask about the mansion?"

"So no one could be living there?" Pacie asked.

"I doubt it. They would have to fix it up or more likely rebuild it, and I don't recall talk of anyone ever doing that." The professor closed the book. "Oh, I forgot to offer you two ladies a cup of tea. Would you like some?"

"No, thank you, Professor," Pacie said. "I don't want to take up your break any longer than necessary."

"It's no problem." The professor stood and walked to the phone on his desk. "Aileen, dear, could you bring in a spot of tea for us?" He walked back to the well-worn couch. "Now where were we?"

"The mansion," Pacie said. "I was trying to figure out if Slenderman could be staying there."

"Slenderman?" The professor adjusted his glasses. "The being made from tulpamancy?"

"I know it sounds crazy, but I think it's what's been abducting children and causing the town's murders."

"Well, there was one rumor that I forgot to mention. When the captain's wife and infant perished, he began to dabble in spiritualism. It was popular and commonly practiced back in those days. If he was successful in the practice, he could've, unwittingly, conjured up something."

"You mean he could've conjured up Slenderman?"

With raised eyebrows, the professor said, "I've never heard talk of Slenderman around here before, but the old captain could've opened a portal or a way to access other dimensions

—if a person were to believe in such things. Slenderman could be an interdimensional being."

"That's what you experienced, Pacie, when you were at the mansion earlier," Irma said. "What do you think?"

"I think you're right."

"So you've been to the mansion?" the professor asked.

Aileen brought a tray of tea into the office and sat it on the coffee table between them. "If you need anything else, let me know."

"Thank you, Aileen," the professor said. "Don't forget to close the door on your way out."

Pacie watched the professor pour hot water into the cups. "Yes, I've been to the mansion and experienced different dimensions. The first one, the mansion was old but in good condition with furniture and things. I remember thinking it would only take a little elbow grease to fix it up. Later when I left and somehow walked in a circle—thanks to a messed up GPS—the mansion looked like it was falling down; it was not the same. But then, it was dark." Pacie put a tea bag in the dainty cup that the professor sat in front of her. "If there is a way to open different dimensions at the mansion, how would I be able to open the one I want? The one that Slenderman is using. I think he might be holding the kids captive in it. How can we get to that dimension?"

Irma bobbed her tea bag in the steaming water and then sat it on the saucer. "I know little about it, but I would not do any spiritualistic rituals or we might end up conjuring something worse than Slenderman. I would suggest walking in the same circle that you did before and see if it brings you into another dimension."

"Sounds like chances of that working is slim," Pacie said.

The professor sat down his tea cup and walked back to the bookshelf where he had retrieved the earlier book. He fumbled around with the contents of a tin box until he found what he was looking for. "This belonged to Captain Perry. It's the original key to the mansion. I believe it's the front door key, but it should unlock other doors as well."

Pacie took the skeleton key that the professor handed her. "This will help us get to the right dimension?"

"I do not know, but it won't hurt to have it with you." The professor sat back down. "I do need it back, however."

"Of course," Pacie said, putting the key into her satchel. "I'll bring it back in a couple of days. We're hoping to go to the mansion tomorrow morning."

"Please be careful," the professor said.

They spoke no more of the mansion nor Captain Perry, but instead of the professor's upcoming trip to Egypt. After hugs and goodbyes, they walked back through the college lobby.

"What's going on out there by the driveway?" Irma said, pointing toward the entrance where students were gathering.

Outside the college, on the sidewalk, was a group of young men taunting and surrounding another student. Pacie and Irma walked outside and watched as water bottles were tossed at the young man, who was surrounded by hooligans.

"Isn't that the kid we talked to when we were investigating the murder on Walnut?" Pacie asked, noting his goth attire.

"You're right. It's the same tall kid with dark clothes," Irma said. "He didn't want to talk to us."

Pacie walked up to a couple of girls who were watching the commotion. "What's going on?"

"They think he's the one abducting kids and murdering people," the girl said.

"They're wrong." Pacie was angry.

Pacie and Irma moved through the crowd that was watching the sight. Shouts of hate and accusations of murder were directed at the young man. Pacie ran up to the kid who wanted to get away, but the mob would not let him go.

"Stop! Don't do this!" Pacie shouted as she ran up and stood next to the student. "He's innocent. He's not the person we're after."

"This is none of your business, Pacie Rose," a male student shouted. He reached down and picked up stones to throw. "He matches the description, and he's new to town. There's no one else who would be doing it."

"It is my business because you have the wrong guy," Pacie said. "I will prove it tomorrow. At least that's my plan."

"And what if you're wrong?" the punk said, tossing stones at them. "This guy will escape."

"You're just going to have to trust me," Pacie said. "Now move away."

Staff from the college came out and dispersed the crowd as a police car drove up.

The battered kid looked at Pacie. "Thanks, but I could've handled this myself."

"I know. I couldn't help myself. I'm the town mystery solver, Pacie Rose."

The kid nodded. "I'm Ray. I am new to town but I'm not

the killer."

Pacie smiled. "I believe you."

"Why am I not surprised to see you here?" Officer Kline said as he walked up. "Seems like you're always where the action is."

"How can I solve crimes if I'm *not* where the action is?" Pacie said. "I'll let you take over from here, Officer Kline."

Pacie caught up with Irma, who was walking to the car.

"Is everything okay over there?" Irma asked.

Pacie put the skeleton key on her keyring.

"Everything's fine." Pacie unlocked the SUV. "Has Haley texted you back?"

Irma looked at her phone. "She didn't say much, other than the suspect's name is Carla Shears. She's a teen and is currently missing. And I know you won't be surprised, but there were unusual markings in the girl's bedroom, similar to the entries in the other teen's journal."

"So that makes two teen suspects who are missing, Carla and Dora. And the kidnapped kids are Morgan and Seth."

"Don't forget Anna and Ben are missing and there are two murder victims, Christine and the elderly woman." Irma let Mr. Dibble back in the SUV. "If we can't stop this tomorrow, there'll be more chaos in town."

"I know," Pacie said, starting the vehicle. "Let's grab a pizza and head home. We'll go to Slenderman's so-called *palace* first thing in the morning and hopefully put an end to all this."

Chapter 23

CHARLOTTE PARKED ON THE dismal Black Water street and looked at the two-story colonial home. She did not feel like babysitting that night. Not just because her friends were going to a movie, one she wanted to see, but she had a sense of foreboding about it. With this crazy man running around town, she did not feel comfortable staying in a stranger's home. Sure, she had babysat for the bratty kids before; even so, there was something wrong.

She grabbed her purse and walked up the driveway to the side door and knocked.

"Hi, Char, come on in," Mrs. Anderson said, holding the door open. "Thanks for babysitting tonight."

"I don't mind," Charlotte said. But she did mind.

"We wouldn't be going anyplace tonight but as I told you on the phone, it's our anniversary and we wanted to do something special."

"I understand," Charlotte said, taking off her shoes. The sweet aroma of cookies filled the air.

Mrs. Anderson pointed to the refrigerator door. "This is

my cell number, which I know you already have. And this is where we'll be, The Villa."

"Thank you, Mrs. Anderson."

The two kids, Bobby and Alice, ran into the kitchen, already dressed in their pajamas.

"Hi Char Char," Alice said, giving her a quick hug around the hip.

"Hi, Alice. How are you?"

"I'm good," she said, running off with Bobby.

"I shouldn't have let them have so much sugar," Mrs. Anderson said.

You're right.

"I made a lot of sweets for my sweet," Mrs. Anderson said, pointing to the counter where two pies, a dish of brownies, and cookies sat. "You can help yourself to it. I think I made too much."

"Thank you. It looks good."

Mr. Anderson came into the kitchen with his jacket draped over his arm. "Hello, Char. Glad you're here. We're in much need of some time to ourselves."

"Congratulations on your anniversary. Have a good time tonight."

"Thank you," Mrs. Anderson said, taking a sweater from the entrance closet. "Kids, we're going."

Bobby and Alice ran back into the kitchen, exchanged kisses with their parents, and then ran out like they were full of piss and vinegar.

"Their bedtime is nine o'clock, and call us if you need anything," Mrs. Anderson said as they walked out the door.

Charlotte locked the kitchen door behind them and watched them get into their car. Then she checked both the front and back doors, making sure they were locked, which they were not.

"Why are you doing that?" Bobby whined. "I want to go outside and play."

"It'll be dark soon, and besides, you have your pajamas on," Charlotte said, closing any open curtains.

Alice walked into the living room with a bag of Barbie dolls. "Can you play dolls with me?"

Charlotte sat on the couch. "Sure."

The hour spent playing Barbies while Bobby played with his cars was over before Charlotte knew it.

"Okay, you guys, bedtime. Put away your toys."

After some grumbles, they brushed their teeth and crawled into bed. Charlotte tucked them in and partially closed their bedroom doors. She walked back down the hallway and stopped at the top of the stairs. For a moment, she thought she heard something moving downstairs, but it was probably the old refrigerator, it did make clicking sounds every once in a while.

Charlotte walked down the staircase, scanning the environment for anything moving, but nothing did.

"I'm not babysitting again until they catch that maniac. It's just not worth it," Charlotte muttered under her breath. She sat on the couch and turned the television to a channel that was not the news, but instead a lighthearted sitcom.

Charlotte jumped when she thought she heard someone trying to come in the back door. It couldn't be Mr. And Mrs.

Anderson because they would use the same side door they had left from. She muted the television and listened. There were no other sounds. Nevertheless, she stood up and walked through the laundry room to the back door. She turned on the porch light and parted the curtain covering the back door's window. She peered out onto the deck and into the backyard. There was no one there. Other than a swing, swinging on its own, as though someone had just been using it. The wind was not blowing. There was nothing to explain the moving swing, and that gave her the creeps. She tested the door again; it was still locked.

When she turned around and looked back toward the living room, the interior of the house seemed darker than it should. It must be her eyes playing tricks on her. She was not sure she wanted to go back there but she could not stay in the laundry room, sitting on top of the dryer for the rest of the time babysitting.

Charlotte looked at her watch; it was nine-thirty. The Anderson's never said what time they would be back, but they usually did not come home until the bar closed, after two o'clock.

She forced herself through the exaggerated fear she felt and went back to the living room and sat down on the couch. She stared at the ridiculous, albeit somewhat funny, television show. At the first commercial, she reached inside her purse and took out her cellphone. There was a text from Grandma Rose telling her to call if she needed anything.

Thanks grandma. I'm a little spooked but things are fine," Charlotte texted back.

Charlotte dropped the phone back inside her purse and sat there, listening for any unusual sounds. She looked at the shadows around the room, deciding she would turn on more lights and disperse the darkness. She turned on nearly all the downstairs lights. There would be no conserving energy tonight.

Before Charlotte sat back down and got comfortable, she would check on the kids. She walked upstairs, not wanting to turn the hallway light on for fear of waking them. The nightlights in the hallway and the kids' bedrooms provided enough light to see if they were fine. She looked in Alice's room first; she was fast asleep with a doll tucked in at her side. Then Charlotte looked in Bobby's bedroom. She jumped when she thought she saw movement in the corner by the closet. Wanting to shine a light in that direction, she reached to her back pocket and realized her phone was downstairs.

Like a stealthy cat, Charlotte walked into Bobby's room and toward the corner where the dark shadow took up occupancy. She reached out her hand and put it into the darkness. The frigid air gave her goosebumps, but she felt nothing physical. It felt like an air conditioner was set on the coldest temperature, but the Andersons did not have central air. It had to be a draft or her mind playing tricks on her.

Knowing the kids were safe, Charlotte went back down to the living room and laid down on the couch. Just a few more hours to go. The kids should sleep the rest of the time.

Charlotte was dosing off when she heard talking. Was it the neighbor? Charlotte sat up. No, it was coming from upstairs. It sounded like Bobby; he must be talking in his sleep. She got up and walked to Bobby's room. She looked in and saw Bobby standing by the bed, talking. He was saying that he would be in trouble if he did whatever was being asked of him. Charlotte turned on the room light. Bobby was talking to himself.

"Who were you talking to?"

"No one," Bobby said, crawling back into bed.

Charlotte walked in and searched the small room thoroughly. It held only Bobby. She tucked him in bed, turned the room light off, and walked back downstairs.

Her stomach growled, indicating it was time for one of the desserts that Mrs. Anderson had baked. Charlotte walked into the kitchen and took a cookie from the glass jar. It was good and the sugar might help her stay awake, even though she wanted to go to sleep. She took a napkin and picked two more cookies and walked back into the living room. She sat on the couch and brought up the television's programming. She stopped searching the guide when she heard Bobby talking again. There's no way he could have gone back to sleep already, so he could not be talking in his sleep. She stopped chewing to listen. The house doors were locked, so no one could have come into the home while she was there. They would have to be inside already.

Charlotte swallowed hard. She sat the napkin of cookies on the coffee table and took the cellphone from her purse. Should she call Mr. and Mrs. Anderson? The police? Maybe Grandma Rose. She thought it best to check on Bobby first because it could be nothing. Bobby could be playing a trick on her; he has done that in the past. Charlotte walked to the staircase and looked up. This time she turned on the staircase lights and walked quietly up the steps, ready to dial 9-1-1.

When she reached the last step, she could see down the hallway; no one was there. No one was talking. Bobby must have gone back to sleep. She went to Alice's door first and peered in—she was still asleep. Then she walked to Bobby's door; he appeared to be sleeping, too. She pushed the door slightly more open and walked inside. She looked around. The hall light cast more light into the room than earlier when only the nightlights did the lighting. There was no one. She knelt, turned on her phone's flashlight, and shined it under the bed. No one there either. The closet was the only place left to check. Part of Charlotte did not want to check the closet and instead grab Bobby and take him downstairs to sleep on the couch—Alice, too. But she had to know if someone else was in the house. With her phone's light still on, she walked to the closet and opened the door, first shining the light low to see if there were legs, legs of the intruder. All she saw were toys, shoes, and clothes that had fallen off their hangers.

Relieved, she turned off her light and walked back to Bobby's bed. He was still sleeping; his breathing was regular. If he was talking earlier, he was doing it in his sleep. Of course, he could be pretending to be asleep, but at least he was in bed with his eyes closed.

Charlotte walked back into the hallway and stood there. If there was someone else in the house, could they be in one of the other rooms? At least the Anderson house was small and not big like Grandma's. She would not rest easy if she did not at least give a cursory look into the rooms. She walked to the master bedroom and turned on the light. She would not look in the closet or under the bed unless she heard something. It was silent. Charlotte switched the light off and checked the bathroom. No one. The only other door must lead to the attic because there was no room for it to be a bedroom. She opened the door. As expected, there was a staircase that led to the attic. She listened. There were no sounds.

Relieved, she went back downstairs and sat on the couch. She slipped her phone into her purse then looked at the cookies, or rather, cookie. Weren't there two cookies left? She had only eaten one of the three she originally had.

Fear shot through her like an electric bolt. There was someone in the house, and now he was downstairs. She might have eaten more, but she was sure she had not.

Then, directly behind her left ear, Charlotte felt an icy breath. Then she heard a gravelly voice say, "Are the children alive?"

Chapter 24

CHARLOTTE SHOT UP AND turned around so fast that she fell onto the coffee table and crashed to the floor. No one was there. There had to be someone hiding behind the couch or the drapes because what she felt and heard was real. But instead of looking, she ran upstairs and into Alice's room. She scooped up the sleeping child from her bed and stood at the door. She peaked around the doorframe, and when she knew the coast was clear, she ran into Bobby's room with the child in her arms.

"What's going on?" Alice asked, clutching her frizzy-haired doll.

Charlotte locked the bedroom door and sat Alice on the bed next to Bobby, who was waking up. Struggling, she pushed the dresser toward the door, inch by inch. Then she realized that she did not have her cellphone.

"Why are you doing that?" Bobby asked, rubbing his eyes as he sat up in bed.

Charlotte said nothing at first as she kept inching the heavy piece of furniture to fully block the door. It might not stop someone from entering, but it would at least slow them down.

"Is there a phone in here, Bobby?"

"No, there's one in mom and dad's room. Are we being robbed?"

"Something like that."

Charlotte shushed the kids and listened. She heard nothing. She looked at the window, wondering what her options were. She could scream and hope someone heard her. She could try to get the three of them to the other bedroom and call the police. Or she could stay put and hope the psycho just went away.

The window opened onto the garage roof. At least if they had to flee, they could go out that way. But then what? Drop the kids to the ground like coyote smugglers dropping kids many feet over the border wall? It was too dangerous to go out the window unless they were forced to.

Charlotte felt her heart racing. Alice was crying and Bobby would not stop talking as Alice clung to him.

"I don't hear anything. Maybe he left," Bobby said.

Charlotte nodded, wondering how Bobby could hear anything with all the noise he was making. But the fact remained, as long as the door was blocked, there was no other way out of the room except by the window.

Charlotte sat next to the kids on the bed. Waiting. No one was banging on the door or turning the doorknob. Maybe he had left, but there was no way she was going to move that dresser to find out. The intruder could be just outside the door, waiting for them.

"Is it the bad guy?" Alice asked.

"I don't know who it is," Charlotte said. "But your parents

will be home soon. We'll just wait here, and everything will be fine."

As the time passed, Charlotte and the kids' anxiety subsided. Alice talked about her doll, Heidi, while Bobby played with action figures.

Charlotte almost died when there were three loud raps at the bedroom window. The kids screamed. Through the partially opened curtain, Charlotte saw the faceless man, and he was trying to lift the sash. Paralyzed with fear for a moment, the screaming of the kids and their shouts to get out, drove her back to the dresser. Charlotte pushed on it so that they could escape through the door, but the legs were stuck on the rug that had rolled up beneath it. All she had to do was move it enough so that they could squeeze out. She tugged on the dresser until there was enough room for her to put her back against the wall and push the chest with her legs. When she looked back at the window, the guy was gone. Was he back in the house and waiting outside the bedroom door?

The kids were screaming to get out of the room, but Charlotte was not going anywhere until she knew where the freak was. For now, it was quiet. She also knew that a strong man could break into this room any time he wanted—dresser or not. And if he were in the house and heard them climbing out the window, he could easily run outside before they figured out a way off the garage roof. But on the other hand, if he were still on the garage roof, she and the kids could run to the parents' bedroom, lock the door, and call the police before he was back inside.

"Bobby, is there a flashlight in your room?" Charlotte asked.

"In the toy box." Bobby rushed to the plastic chest and pushed toys aside until he found a big plastic toy flashlight. "Here it is."

Charlotte took it from Bobby. "Does it work?"

"The batteries are probably dead."

The flashlight did not turn on. Charlotte tried to open the battery compartment but because it was a toy, she needed a small Philips-head screwdriver to gain access. "Do you have tools, like a screwdriver?"

Bobby shrugged. "I don't think so. Dad has a screwdriver in his toolbox."

"Do you have a toolbox in here?" Charlotte thought it was worth asking.

He shook his head, then fished through the toy box again, and this time brought out a large plastic screwdriver. "Will this work?"

"It's too big."

Charlotte first tried to use her fingernail to turn the screw, but it was too tight. "I need something to take this screw out. Something with a pointy tip to it."

Charlotte went through the toy box with Bobby and Alice. They kept holding up useless items. Then she found an expired credit card that the parents probably were letting him play with. Using a corner of the card she was able to open the flashlight and remove two C-batteries."

"Now I need working batteries. Does anything else in this room take these batteries?"

They looked around the room; there was nothing else that took batteries or could be used to shine out the window. She dropped the flashlight back into the toy box and stood there with her hands on her hips.

"What are you thinking?" Bobby asked.

"I was going to use the flashlight to shine it outside, but I guess we'll just have to keep the bedroom light on so that it shines out the window and then we can see what's out there."

"I don't want to open the window," Alice said.

"Not open the window, just the curtain. You two can stand aside like in that corner and I'll look."

"Wait," Bobby said, taking the big plastic screwdriver from the toy box. He held it out for Charlotte to take. "You need a weapon."

"Ah, good idea, Bobby," Charlotte said, taking the screwdriver from Bobby's hand. "Okay, stand in that corner over there."

Charlotte walked to the curtain, looked at the kids, and forced a reassuring smile. She parted the dark green panels by only an inch. Nothing moved, so she slid the curtains farther aside.

"What do you see?" Bobby asked.

"Not much."

"Do you see the bad guy?" Alice asked, keeping her doll close to her chest.

"No, I don't." The only thing Charlotte knew for sure was that the maniac was not directly in front of the window.

"Is he in the house?" Bobby asked, walking to Charlotte.

"Maybe he left," Charlotte said, trying to sound optimistic.

"Turn the bedroom light on and off, like a code," Bobby said, looking out the window.

"That's a good idea, but your neighbors are too far away, and no one is awake to see it. I don't see lights on anywhere."

"We can scream and maybe they would hear us," Alice said.

"Another good idea but we would have to open the window and I'm not sure I want to do that."

"I saw something move," Bobby said.

"Where?"

Before Bobby could point out the movement, the faceless man slammed against the pane of glass, almost breaking it.

Bobby screamed and ran to the dresser, blocking the door.

"Let's get out of here." Charlotte put the plastic screwdriver in her back pocket. She moved the dresser a little more away from the door, allowing them just enough room to escape.

Bobby squeezed between the dresser and door first.

"Run to your parents' room."

Alice was next through the tight space.

"Follow your brother."

Charlotte was beginning to panic because as far as she could tell, the guy was not at the window anymore, so he had to be coming inside. She pressed her body through the narrow space and sprinted to the parents' bedroom, locking the door behind her. A large bureau was on the other side of the room, and it looked to be too heavy for her to move.

"Bobby, help me with the bed. We should be able to move it enough to block the door. Alice, call nine-one-one."

Alice ran into the closet in fear instead.

When the bed blocked the door, Charlotte ran to the phone and dialed 9-1-1. She gave them the needed information while staying on the phone.

"We can't go out this window," Bobby said, "because we're too high."

Then Charlotte noticed there was another door; it must go into the bathroom. There was no choice; the heavy bureau was going to have to be moved to keep the bathroom door closed.

"Bobby, help me with the dresser," Charlotte said, locking the bathroom door. She rushed to the enormous chest of drawers and used more force than she ever used before just to budge the thing. Even Bobby was grunting as he gave it his all. Even though they were out of sync with their pushing and pulling, they managed to move it inch by inch, but it was taking too long. The mirror was attached at the base; there was no removing it without the proper tools, so she took out the drawers to lighten it, throwing them on the floor.

Then the bathroom doorknob jiggled. The intruder was in there. Bobby screamed and joined Alice in the closet.

"The police are on the way," Charlotte said with authority. "They'll be here any minute."

Charlotte kept pushing on the monstrous piece of furniture as delicate glass perfume bottles toppled over, releasing a floral aroma of lilacs and roses. Finally, she had at least a part of the bureau in front of the bathroom door. Then whatever was on the other side broke the lock. The door slammed into the back of the dresser, leaving a gap of a few inches; not enough for the guy to get through.

Charlotte screamed when she thought she saw a snake or an octopus tentacle move through the opening, reaching for her. She took the toy screwdriver from her back pocket and began stabbing at it.

Sirens sounded in the background.

"I hear the police sirens, they're almost here," Charlotte shouted.

The man laughed a maniacal laugh. "This is not over, Charlotte Booth. But if you want to earn a reward and visit my palace, all you have to do is give me the children."

"Never gonna happen!"

"There are consequences for denying me." The man laughed.

"Who are you," Charlotte said with anger.

The kids whimpered while Charlotte waited for an answer that never came. The wonderful sound of the police entering the home and charging upstairs reassured her that the worst was over.

"We're in here," Charlotte called out, not wanting to open any doors until she knew for sure it was safe.

"This is the police. Are you okay in there?" an officer bellowed on the other side of the door.

The kids ran to Charlotte, ready to be saved.

"We're fine. Just need to move some furniture. Bobby, help me move the bed," Charlotte said, dropping the screwdriver.

Charlotte opened the door and officers came into the room.

"Is he gone?" Charlotte asked, holding the kids' hands.

Detective Wanat walked into the room. "We're searching the house now."

"I'm sure glad to see you, Haley," Charlotte said, feeling safe for the first time since she walked into the Andersons' home. "He was in the bathroom. I stabbed a slimy tentacle thing that he was pushing through the door with that plastic screwdriver on the floor over there. There could be blood or something on it to test."

"I'm relieved you and the kids are alright." Det. Wanat smiled and looked at the kids. "We called your parents, and they are on their way home. They should be here at any time."

Bobby let go of Charlotte's hand. "Char and me moved the dressers to keep the burglar out."

"You did an outstanding job," Det. Wanat said as she directed officers to inspect the area by the bathroom door. "Your parents will be proud of you."

Charlotte sat on the bed with Alice next to her. "As if the tentacle wasn't bad enough, but this guy said some strange things to me."

Detective Wanat paused, then said, "What did he say?'

Charlotte was surprised at Det. Wanat's serious, almost distressed tone. "First of all, he knew my name. And he said that if I gave him the children that I would get a reward and could live in his palace."

"What did you say to that?"

"I said it wasn't gonna happen. Then he said there are consequences for not doing what he says. That really freaked me out."

"Did you get a look at him?"

Charlotte was not sure how to answer the question without sounding crazy, but she had already mentioned the tentacle. "Well, he was in the dark outside Bobby's window, but he looked tall and thin and his face—" Charlotte shook her head. "His face, I couldn't really see it. He must've had a mask or something on because I saw no eyes or mouth. He had no facial features. Oh, and he must've had a key to the house, or he was already inside when I got here because all the doors were locked."

"Have you spoken with your grandma Pacie since this started?"

"No, not yet. But I will."

Mrs. Anderson called for Alice and Bobby as she ran up the staircase and down the hall to the bedroom. She dropped to her knees and embraced the children. "Oh, my god. Are you guys alright?"

"You can take them downstairs," Det. Wanat said.

As Mrs. and Mr. Anderson helped the kids out of the bedroom, Mr. Anderson turned to Charlotte. "Thanks for taking good care of Alice and Bobby. We should never have asked you to babysit while a killer was out there. It won't happen again."

Charlotte stood up as the Anderson family left the room. "Is it alright if I go home now?"

Detective Wanat smiled. "Just a few more questions, then you're free to go. We'll also have a patrol car monitor your home since that guy knew your name."

After giving the police all the details she could remember, Charlotte thanked Det. Wanat and walked to the bedroom door. Her legs and arms were shaking so much she had to hold on to the doorframe for a moment. "I can't stop shaking."

"It's a delayed stress reaction; it happens to us all. Do you need help downstairs?"

"No, I'll be fine. I'm just glad it's all over."

❧❧❧

The ringing of the cellphone on the nightstand woke Pacie up. Her first thoughts were that Mr. Dibble needed to go outside. She looked at the clock, it was after midnight.

"Yeah?"

"Pacie." Irma sounded frantic. "Where was Char babysitting tonight?"

Fear of another murder shot through Pacie. "The Anderson's, I think. Why?"

"That's on Oak Street, isn't it?"

"I believe so."

"My police scanner just went off and something has happened there. We gotta go there now."

Pacie at once hung up and rushed to Irma's room. She unlocked the door and went inside. "Are you sure it's the same place?"

"I don't know exactly what place it is," Irma said as she dressed, sliding her jeans out from under Mr. Dibble, who was lying on them in the chair.

"I'm getting dressed, then we can go over there," Pacie said, rushing to her room. She dressed, ran a comb through her hair, and grabbed her satchel.

"I'm putting Mr. Dibble outside for a moment," Irma shouted as she headed for the staircase.

Pacie was right behind her. "I'll be in the car."

The garage door opened and Pacie backed out into the driveway. She rolled down her window. The air was damp, and fog still floated in layers through the air. Moments later,

Irma and Mr. Dibble were inside the car.

Irma sat her backpack on the floor and took a cigarette from her pouch. She was about to light it when she remembered she did not want to taint the effects of reconciliation and what they had to do to stop Slenderman. "I can't believe this is happening."

"Me either," Pacie said as she wiped her sweaty palms on her pant legs. "Did you hear any details?"

"Just that there was an intruder in the house and that there was a female and two children there."

Pacie did not want to ask, but she had to know, "That sounds just like Char. Did it say anything about—anyone being hurt?"

"Thank goodness, no."

Pacie drove faster than she should have to the house. It was easy to find because of the police activity around it. She drove up and parked as close as the police would allow. "We should call Amanda."

"I'll do it," Irma said.

Pacie got out of the car and walked into the barrage of red and blue lights. She saw Det. Wanat and Charlotte walking out of the house and jogged up to them. "Char, are you okay? Are the kids fine?"

"I'm fine and they're fine, but I'm not babysitting again until that maniac is caught."

"Good idea. I don't want you to."

Irma ran up to them. "I called your mom."

"Thanks, but I already called her. And I was wondering if you guys can follow me home?"

"We will," Irma said.

"You know," Charlotte said, "there is something strange about all this."

"What is that?" Det. Wanat asked.

"The guy could somehow move from one place to another super fast. I mean, one minute he was at the window and the next he was inside the house. It's like he was a ghost and could go through walls."

"Maybe there were two of them," Pacie said, even though she believed what Charlotte was saying.

"This is freaking me out. It seemed like the same guy but if there were two of them..." Charlotte shivered.

Pacie looked at Det. Wanat. "Can I speak with you a moment?"

"Mr. Dibble would like to say hi," Irma said to Charlotte. "He's in the car."

As Irma and Charlotte walked away, Pacie said, "What happened?"

Detective Wanat described the events. "There's no evidence so far, other than Charlotte's description. And we're no closer to finding the killer."

"Are you going to be by your phone today?" Pacie asked.

"Yes. Why?" Det. Wanat crossed her arms. "What trouble are you two going to get into today?"

Pacie smiled weakly. "Nothing. Just wondering."

Chapter 25

RELIEVED CHARLOTTE WAS ABLE to thwart Slenderman, Pacie and Irma went back to the mansion and got a couple of hours of shut-eye. Hoping to get an early start on their quest for the mansion in the woods, they would rise before the sun was up.

Irma and Mr. Dibble came downstairs as the birds began their early morning melody. She set her backpack on the kitchen floor and poured herself a cup of coffee.

Pacie was already sitting at the table, sipping coffee and eating toast that was smothered in the strawberry jam they had made. "Are you ready for this?"

Irma sat down. "I am. My phone and video camera batteries are charged, and I have extra batteries. Even a hat to keep the bugs away. Have you told anyone what we're doing today?"

"No, but I asked Haley if she was going to be by her phone today."

"How about Johnny?"

"No, I'm waiting. If I tell him too soon, he'll talk me out of it."

"I want Mr. Dibble to come with us."

"Not a problem. He does have a good nose."

"For some things, like squirrels and groundhogs. But his bite is what I'm thinking about. It could come in handy for defeating the bad guys."

Pacie finished her slice of toast. "I think what we'll do is park as Sugar Sand and walk back to it the same—or relatively the same—path that I took last time. Hopefully, the mansion isn't a pile of rotting lumber. I want to walk inside and inspect things. But when I was there before it wasn't brand new, and Slenderman or the kids were not there."

"So it needs to be new, like someone was living there. In Dora's journal, she wrote that Slenderman said she could live in his palace. But that house isn't a palace, is it?"

"No, it's just a big old house."

"So we could be barking up the wrong tree."

"We could be. If we are, then I don't know where else to go."

"We'll find out."

"What about the crucifix Father gave you and the skeleton key from the professor? How exactly are we going to use them?"

"I don't know. We'll figure that out as we go along."

"Don't forget to take them."

"I already have the crucifix around my neck and the key is on the keyring with my other keys."

As the morning light cast a dull gray hue into the kitchen, and when they finished breakfast, Pacie grabbed two flannel shirts from her closet and an old baseball cap that belonged to Patrick to keep the bugs off, just in case they needed it. They went out to the SUV and began their journey to Sugar Sand Park. Not surprisingly, the fog had not been burned off by the rising sun, but instead hung thick in the early morning air.

"It's hard to see through this haze, but it looks like storm clouds could be heading our way," Irma said, looking west over Lake Michigan.

"We might get wet but there's no turning back," Pacie said.

"Don't worry," Irma said, "I don't want to turn around."

Pacie pulled into the parking lot and the three of them got out of the SUV. Pacie tied a flannel shirt around her waist and put a heavy coating of bug spray on before donning the Blue Stars cap. Even Mr. Dibble got a coating of spray. She put her satchel crossbody, dropped the keyring into the bag, and put her cellphone in the back pocket of her jeans. "Ready?"

"Let's do it," Irma said, as she adjusted the backpack straps.

The three walked to the trail, still with yellow police line tape across its entry. Down the path they went with Mr. Dibble at their heels. They were feeling confident, armed with their arsenal.

When they turned left at the fork, Pacie looked down and saw the rabbit and its twisted neck still alongside the trail. "I can't believe animals haven't dragged that rabbit away."

"It's like mutilated cows," Irma said. "Predators won't eat cows that have had body parts mysteriously removed. It's like they know the cow is contaminated or something."

When they reached the spot where Pacie had left the trail last time, Pacie said, "Here is where I left the trail. It's rough going with the raspberries and bugs."

"Let's go."

They left the trail and slogged through the brambles. Pacie put on the flannel shirt that she had around her waist, not because of the bugs, but because it kept getting snagged on thorns.

They walked for what felt like all morning, but was closer to an hour, when Pacie said, "We're almost there."

They walked ahead through thinning trees until they arrived in the clearing where Captain Perry's dilapidated mansion sat.

"Wow, it is a big house, but it's not a palace and it's not new," Irma said, in awe of the massive building. "It doesn't look new. Does this mean we have to walk in a circle now?"

"I guess so. Follow me."

Pacie guessed where she had left the grounds the other night in the dark and had somehow circled back to the mansion. She looked at her phone. "I guess we should follow the phone's GPS because the last time I followed it, it looked like I was going in a straight line but was actually circling back to the mansion. If I'm wrong, the worst that'll happen is that it'll take us back to the park."

"Just do what you did last time," Irma said.

"Okay, I'll follow the GPS like I want to go back to the car. I just hope we don't end up there. We have kids to save."

Back into the dense woods they went. Distant thunder rumbled as they spent time walking, time they did not want to use.

"We must be coming back out to the trail," Irma said. "The trees aren't as thick."

"I'm not so sure," Pacie said.

When they got to what looked like the clearing of a trail, was in reality the clearing of the land that the mansion sat on. The new mansion.

"I can't believe this," Irma said as she pulled an old dry burr from around Mr. Dibble's ear. "It's like we stepped into another dimension or another time, but we didn't go through a portal. I know this is what we were hoping for but it's still unbelievable."

"We can figure that science stuff out later. Right now, we have to destroy Slenderman," Pacie said, standing there, staring at the grand old home that should not be there.

"Did it look like this when you went inside last time," Irma asked, recording it with her video camera.

"No. It wasn't a pile of lumber like we saw earlier, and it wasn't brand new like this. It was in between. But it did look brand new when I came back around in the dark after I left."

"Let's walk around the outside first," Irma said. "I want to see if there are cars or a driveway or someone else here."

"I wouldn't be surprised if we see a horse and carriage," Pacie said. "We'll need to be quiet, I don't want Slenderman knowing we're here."

They began walking around the exterior of the old captain's mansion. It was easy to see that he loved his pregnant wife and was putting great care into the home's construction. Mr. Dibble sniffed along the stone foundation but was jumping back at the slightest of movements. Drapes were open, and a woody wisteria vined its way up the side of the structure, its purplish flowers drooping for show. The two-track path was on the south side of the house. It left Irma wondering what would happen if they were to walk down it. Would they get trapped in this dimension or walk out of it into normal time?

"It looks like someone lives here," Pacie said.

"Look." Irma pointed to a small barn where a corralled white pony watched them. "We've gone back in time. When did the professor say the house was built?"

"I think he said eighteen-ninety-five."

"Is it possible that there's a second house back here?"

"A house that no one knows about?"

"I'm having trouble believing what I'm seeing."

Pacie nodded. "I know; me too. But it is real. Let's get to work."

Fog hung around the house like a blanket and the air smelled of rain. Pacie stood at the porch steps and looked at the closed front door. "Ready to go inside?"

"Not really. But if we don't get a roof over our heads, we're going to get wet." Irma motioned for Mr. Dibble to follow them.

They walked up the steps and stood at the door. Pacie whispered, "That's the same lion's head doorknocker, just newer and shinier."

"It feels like we should knock," Irma whispered.

Pacie walked along the porch to the same windows she had looked in the last time she was there. They were clean and she could see inside. The furniture had no dust coverings. While it looked like someone could be living there, there were no signs of human occupation like dirty dishes or half-eaten fast food. It was like the captain had straightened things in the home before setting out on a voyage.

Pacie walked back to the door and turned the knob. The door opened with no creaks and she did not need to use her body weight to push on it. She stepped inside onto the swept floor. There were no sounds of people or children.

Irma recorded their entry into the house, then whispered, "Is it possible that only objects can be transported through time and not people?"

"I have no idea."

"What if it morphs to another time with us inside? Do we go with it?"

"Again, I have no idea. I just hope we find the kids and get out of here before there is a change."

With Mr. Dibble following behind, they searched the first floor.

"It doesn't look like a killer lives here," Irma said. "Or anyone else for that matter."

"I know," Pacie said, walking back to the staircase. "But that doesn't mean someone won't come back. We need to hurry."

They searched the second floor, finding nothing different from what they had found downstairs. Until—

"Ah, Pacie, I think you need to take a look at this," Irma said, standing in front of a bedroom door.

Pacie walked up to her and peered into the bedroom. Her breath halted as if the act of drawing in air would give her away. She backed away from the door, pulling Irma by the arm. "The bedsheets are messed up. Someone has been sleeping in there."

"Where are they? And when are they coming back?"

"Or—" Pacie went to a room she had already looked at for signs of the children. "Oh, my god. This room has a half-made bed and clothes draped over the back of a chair. It was not this way a moment ago."

"We're morphing into another dimension. We should stay close to each other so that if things change again, we move through it together."

"Good idea," Pacie said. She looked down at Mr. Dibble, who was standing next to them. "Make sure he doesn't wander off. I don't want us to get separated and possibly enter different dimensions."

"I should've brought my leash."

"We have to get moving and find where it looks like the kids are being held before we move into the dimension where people are physically present and taken prisoner or something worse," Pacie said. "I suggest we quickly check the attic and then go to the basement. I didn't check the basement the last time, so I don't know what's down there."

The attic revealed nothing of significance. When they went back down to the second floor, Irma looked at the bedrooms. One bedroom had a bed that was now made, and the other had clothes folded in the chair that were previously draped over the chairback.

"Pacie, it's like we're ghosts to each other. The people are here moving things—we just can't see them and they can't see us."

"And we won't be able to see the kids, only cages or ropes or things that would restrain a person."

"Until we are in the right time, the right dimension," Irma said.

"Well, if it keeps cycling, then we'll eventually see who it is.

This could be Ben and Anna's room for all we know."

They hurried back downstairs to the door that looked like it led to the basement. Pacie turned the knob and pulled the door open. A staircase led downward into darkness. Pacie felt for a light switch but found none, so she turned on her phone's flashlight while Irma turned on the light of her video camera. They walked cautiously down the rickety wooden steps to the dirt floor of the basement.

"Cages," Pacie said, looking at three dog pens. "They're empty. If the kids are in there, they can't even stand up."

"They might hold the kids, but they could also be holding ferocious dogs. Or they could simply be empty cages, too."

"The way I feel about this whole thing right now, I'm inclined to believe they're holding the kidnapped kids," Pacie said.

"I wonder if they can see our lights?" Irma said, recording as she shined the camera light on the cages. Dog dishes and a kitty litter box were in each.

Before they could work on opening the metal mesh enclosures, a ghostly lantern and creaking steps caught their attention. They turned off their lights and stood there, as still as any ghost that would be hiding. Seeing no people, it was possible a child was scared and shouted for help when they saw Pacie and Irma's moving lights when no people were holding them.

Pacie wondered what would happen if the person who came downstairs walked into them. Would they bump into each other, or would the person simply pass right through them? Right now, there was no contact.

Irma knelt and began petting Mr. Dibble, trying to keep

him from moving and disturbing the soil on the floor.

There were no sounds of people talking, and none of the cage doors opened as the floating lantern went from cage to cage and then back up the staircase, closing the door behind them.

As far as Pacie remembered, they had not moved anything, aside from opening the door and not closing it.

"I wonder if the people here know that the dimensions are shifting," Irma said.

"I hope not, otherwise they'll be waiting for us to slide into their dimension where we'd be visible—then we'll be in one of those cramped cages." Pacie looked around the room. "There's enough light coming in the basement windows for us to see so I suggest we keep our lights off so that we don't call more people down here."

"Let's set on those boxes over there and wait for the next change," Irma said.

They moved and sat down as quietly as possible so as not to frighten the kids in the cages—if they were kids in the cages.

"Whoever came down here did not seem to notice a floating video camera or my phone," Pacie said.

"Maybe it was too dark," Irma said.

"But they would have surely noticed our clothes standing upright," Pacie said. "I mean, we could see their clothes, but not see them."

"Maybe there's a several-inch or one-foot barrier around living things," Irma said. "So things like my backpack and your purse fall within that space, but we did see the floating lantern."

"Following your hypothesis, the person holding the lantern

probably had their arm outstretched and outside the invisible cloak surrounding us."

Irma nodded. "That makes sense. But what if the dimensions go so far back, like before the house was built and the basement dug, could we end up buried underground?"

The whole thing felt surreal as thunder rumbled outside the mansion walls and flashes of light shot through the basement windows, illuminating the bygone furnace and its many arms of ducts that would surely come to life like a Frankenstein octopus if lightning were to strike the mansion.

They waited for what felt like hours but was only thirty minutes. Mr. Dibble woke from his nap, wanting to leave the basement, but Irma held him back.

"Something's happening," Pacie said, standing up.

"Look," Irma said, pointing to the cages. "Shapes are forming."

"Let's stay together," Pacie said, grabbing hold of Irma's hand while Irma put an arm around Mr. Dibble.

"We're changing," Irma said. "We're going through another dimensional shift."

"And I'll bet the kids will start screaming when they see us," Pacie said, tightening her grip on Irma's hand.

Chapter 26

PACIE COULD NOT TAKE her eyes off the cages as forms of two children began to take shape. One cage held Morgan, taken from the playground by Slenderman, and the other cage held Seth taken from the bible study by Ben and Anna.

"Shhh," Pacie said, moving slowly toward the children stuffed inside the wire mesh boxes. "Don't scream, we're here to help you and get you back home."

The kids cowered in the corner of their cage, whimpering as if they had digressed back to an infantile stage or worse yet, like trapped animals. The stench of urine was strong, and the sight of bloody wounds on their legs made Pacie sick.

"How are we getting them out of here?" Irma said, pulling on a lock that secured a chain around the door.

Pacie looked at the child in the first cage. "Are you Morgan?"

The wild-haired girl nodded.

"Are you Seth?" Pacie said, looking over at the boy, crouching back against what had to be miserably hard steel bars.

The boy did not answer.

"Morgan, do you know where they keep the key to these

locks?"

Morgan's arm trembled as she pointed toward the staircase.

Pacie went to the stairs and used her phone for light. There was a hook at the bottom step holding a ring of keys. She took the keys and began fumbling through them, trying to free young Seth first.

"I'm gonna try to find a back door or some other way to get out of here," Irma said.

"Call the police first."

"I've already tried but my phone won't work."

There were a dozen keys on the ring; all Pacie needed was two of them. She was so frenzied from the rush of freeing the kids that she kept dropping them onto the floor. Finally, she found the one that opened Seth's cell. She unwrapped the chain and slid it through the bars, knowing it was making too much noise as it clanked on the metal. She opened the door. "Come out, Seth. Now."

The reluctant lad barely was able to crawl through the door. Pacie helped Seth climb the rest of the way out. She felt his rib bones through his skin. Was he normally this skinny or had he not been fed much, if anything during the time he was missing? Probably both.

Morgan had moved up to the door, waiting for her chance to be rescued. When Pacie found the right key, Morgan left the pen on feeble limbs, sobbing.

"Irma, did you find a way out?" Pacie said, leaving the key in the lock. She took the kids by the hand and walked to the far corner of the basement where she could see Irma's light.

"There's an old coal shoot, but I bet it's locked on the

outside. Other than that, there are basement windows," Irma said. "Or the basement door and hope no one's around."

"I don't like any of them," Pacie said. "Why can't things ever be easy?"

"I'm gonna see if I can get through the window," Irma said.

Irma stacked decaying books on top of an old desk. She climbed on top of the unstable pile and began pushing and pulling on the window while Pacie held a light so that she could see what she was doing. "I can't open this unless we break the glass. And if I break the glass, it will leave sharp pieces. Plus it will be noisy."

"Let's try the coal chute. Watch the kids," Pacie said, walking over by the ancient furnace. She climbed onto the bin where unused coal still lay on the bottom and grabbed hold of the metal chute. She tried to pull herself up, but it was slippery and there was little to hold on to.

"I'll help you. And Mr. Dibble, you watch the kids," Irma said, pushing on Pacie's legs.

Pacie kept sliding backward on the slick sheet metal. Finally, Irma could hold Pacie in place long enough for her to push on the door. "It's not opening."

"I'm not surprised. I thought it'd be locked on the outside," Irma said.

Pacie slid back down to the floor. "I guess that leaves the basement door. You carry Seth and I'll carry Morgan."

They made their way to the bottom of the steps.

"I don't hear anyone moving around up there," Irma said.

"We'd better get going on this before it gets dark," Pacie said, setting down Morgan. "I can't carry you up the steps so hold my hand and follow me."

When Pacie reached the top of the door, and after a moment of listening, she turned the knob so slowly that if anyone were outside looking at the door, they would not notice it. Then she pushed the door open a crack. Inside the hallway, a dark gray tint filled the air. Pacie heard Irma tell the kids to be quiet as she opened the door farther. She stepped from the landing into the hallway. She could hear no one. The backdoor was straight down the hall.

Pacie motioned for Morgan to come to her and stand next to her. Irma, still carrying Seth, was next, with Mr. Dibble bringing up the rear. Pacie quietly closed the door and put a finger over her lips as she pointed toward the backdoor.

Irma nodded and took Morgan by the hand, adjusted Seth on her hip, and doddered down the long hallway toward the door where the storm raged on the other side. She looked back at Pacie.

Pacie nodded the go-ahead then watched Irma release the children and then struggle to open the door.

Irma looked back at Pacie and held up her hands, then mouthed, "It won't open."

Remembering the skeleton key that the professor had given her, Pacie took her keyring from the satchel and tossed it to Irma, who could not catch it. The keys fell to the floor with a flourish of clinks. So much for being quiet.

After struggling with the lock way too long, Irma could finally turn the knob and open the door. She tossed the keys back to Pacie, who also could not catch it. If they were not in such dire straits, Pacie would have made a joke about softball not being their forte. She picked up the keyring. Then from behind Pacie, directly behind her, was the evilest voice of phlegm mixed with gravel that she had ever heard. "Where do you think you are going, Pacie Rose?"

Pacie spun around. It was Slenderman. It was tall but had its head bent down so that its face was inches in front of Pacie's. And just as everyone had described, this pale-faced freak had no eyes, no nose, not even a mouth. How it spoke to her, and where its foul breath emanated from, she did not know.

"Get away from us," Pacie screamed. She looked back at Irma. "Get the kids to safety. I'll catch up with you."

Irma rushed out the back door and into the downpour, practically dragging Morgan with Seth still on her hip, clinging to Irma for dear life. Mr. Dibble stood beside Pacie, barking at the threat.

"Do you want to live in my palace, Pacie Rose? I will reward you with riches beyond your wildest dreams. All you have to do is bring back the children."

"You're a lunatic. I would never live here with you. And this is not a palace."

"I have made the offer, and you have refused it?"

"Damned right." Pacie remembered the crucifix Father had given her. She pulled on the chain under her shirt with the oversized crucifix, but it was snagged on her brassiere.

Slenderman laughed like that of a madman suffering from a sick state of mind.

Pacie began backing toward the exit while Slenderman kept pace with her and began reaching for her neck. Mr. Dibble leapt toward the entity's neck, but the Goliath of a thing swatted him against the wall.

Slenderman was stronger than he looked, and she had doubts she could escape. Until she freed the crucifix, pulling it out from under her shirt with one smooth action. Pacie held it out in front of the ghoul's face. To her amazement, it repelled Slenderman and made him step back—if you could call his floating nature a step. Mr. Dibble attacked again, this time Slenderman flung him back several feet, causing him to slide on the wood floor and slam into a wall.

Pacie kept the crucifix aimed at the thing's faceless head and kept backing up.

"You can't escape, Pacie Rose." Slenderman turned his head to the side as if avoiding a blinding welder's flash and its radiation.

Pacie wanted to destroy this thing, but she did not know how. All she could do was keep it from strangling her, a task it sincerely wanted to complete. Father never said what to do if she were to encounter such a situation but, in the movies, they recite The Lord's Prayer. What could it hurt? Instead of continuing her retreat, she began moving toward Slenderman as she recited the prayer and kept the crucifix extended in front of her as though it were a shield. And it seemed to bother the skinny, cowering thing.

Mr. Dibble pounced again. This time Slenderman could not break the grip of the dog's powerful jaws as it bit into its neck.

Pacie saw Slenderman weakening while snakelike append-ages flailed from his back. But he was still there and still a threat. If she and Mr. Dibble stopped their resistance, he would regain his strength—and that would be that. She did not want to touch the awful, inhuman thing, but she pushed the crucifix against Slenderman's forehead while Mr. Dibble worked to break its spindly neck. As soon as the silvery metal contacted whatever this thing's skin was made of, Slenderman instantly vanished in a puff of stinking sulfur smoke. It was gone.

Mr. Dibble stood in place and looked around as if confused.

"It worked." Pacie smiled as she knelt and hugged Mr. Dibble. "We did it."

But now there was the matter of a furious Anna and Ben who had been standing far behind Slenderman. She did not want to deal with them; they were human—more vulnerable to a gunshot wound than a crucifix. But it did not matter because she had no gun with her. Fortunately, they seemed as surprised by Slenderman's disappearance as she was. Escape was her only thought.

Pacie shouted for Mr. Dibble to follow her as she ran to the backdoor, left open by Irma, and shot out of it like a peregrine falcon during a hunting stoop. She flew down the back steps and could tell by the fuzzy rain that the dimension was changing again. When she reached the ground, she fell to her hands and knees. She looked back at the house; it was no longer perfect. Instead, it stood there, or rather, balanced itself on rotting walls, ready to collapse.

Pacie stood up and called for Mr. Dibble. He was not there. Had he not made it out of the house before the transition?

Chapter 27

PACIE STILL HELD HER keyring as she looked around. Aside from Mr. Dibble being missing, Irma and the kids were nowhere to be found either. Odds were good that they had made it safely away from the house and were not stuck in another dimension. She walked up the rickety back steps and tried to open the back door, but the weight of the house on the doorframe allowed it to open only about a foot.

Doubting Ben and Anna, as well as Slenderman, were in this dimension Pacie called for Mr. Dibble. He did not come running as she hoped. She did not dare try to squeeze through the door and go inside because it appeared the house was about to collapse.

Pacie stayed several feet away from the house as she walked around it to the front door. The rain soaked her as it streamed down her face. To collect her thoughts and figure out how she was going to find Mr. Dibble, Pacie walked up the squishy porch steps and stood under the sagging porch roof. She wiped rainwater from her face and thought about what she could do next before running back into the woods—without

Mr. Dibble.

She began to put the keys back into her satchel when the skeleton key glowed from a lightning flash as if it were trying to tell her something. She turned and looked at the front door as she singled out the skeleton key. Wind sprayed rain against her as she walked up to the front door and tried to turn the resistant doorknob. She put the skeleton key into the lock and turned it. The door opened and as it did a new dimension developed before her, one from a time when the mansion stood strong. Its timbers strengthened and the floorboards stiffened. It made no sense, but nothing made sense anyway.

Pacie called for Mr. Dibble, but he did not come. Neither did Anna nor Ben. Instead of going inside and searching, she closed the door and locked it with the key. Then she inserted the skeleton key again and unlocked the door. When she opened the door this time, Anna was standing directly in front of her.

"Hey, sweetie," Anna said snidely. "Here for your mutt?"

Pacie was mad at herself for not planning to have her pocketknife ready. "I'm not here for you, Anna. I just want my dog."

"That's too bad," Anna said, snapping her gum. "Because we're here for you. You destroyed our messiah and now we must destroy you."

Pacie could see Ben holding Mr. Dibble's collar, not allowing him to move. She knew Mr. Dibble could escape from Ben by attacking him as he did with Slenderman, but he was trained to not harm humans unless he thought his Master Irma or she was in danger. "I want my dog and then we'll be out of here."

Before Pacie could react, Anna had grabbed Pacie's hair and pulled her inside. Mr. Dibble began barking. The keys were still in Pacie's hand. She gripped the skeleton key like a dagger and plunged it into Anna's face as hard as she could.

Anna screamed and released her grip on Pacie's hair. Anna put her hands on her bloody face. "The bitch just poked out my eye."

Mr. Dibble broke free from Ben and ran to Pacie while Ben went to Anna's aid.

Pacie and Mr. Dibble had just crossed the front door threshold when Ben came at them with a butcher knife. Pacie tried closing the door, but Ben stopped it with his foot. He thrust his arm through the opening, slashing the air with the blade, catching Pacie's arm.

Pacie yelled in pain as she kept pushing on the door, trying to close it. Mr. Dibble began gnawing on Ben's stocking foot, causing him to back away, but not before Mr. Dibble received a gash to the top of his head. Pacie closed the door with a whack and used the blood-stained skeleton key to lock it, hoping it would send them to another dimension or, at the very least, delay them in their pursuit of her and Mr. Dibble.

The dimension turned, leaving the kidnappers, and the rain, behind.

Pacie and Mr. Dibble raced through the woods as fast as they could go until they reached the trail and the park, where they caught the attention of the police.

Exhausted, Pacie dropped to her knees as Det. Wanat ran up to her.

"What happened?" Det. Wanat asked.

"I think I just killed Slenderman."

"Who?"

"The child abductor and murderer." Pacie looked toward the parking lot where a couple of ambulances sat. "Are the kids and Irma alright?"

"They're fine; Irma called us. And you both are bleeding; you and the dog," Det. Wanat said, examining Pacie's arm and Mr. Dibble's head. She got on her walkie-talkie and called the paramedics.

"Thank god everyone's fine," Pacie said, still breathing heavy.

"You and Irma did good today."

Pacie nodded. "Mr. Dibble did good, too."

"Yeah." Haley looked down at the panting dog. "You said you killed the perp. Did you happen to see the accomplices?"

"I saw Ben and Anna. I ended up poking out one of Anna's eyes to escape. But I didn't see the other two, Dora and Carla."

"Any deaths, other than the person you call Slenderman?"

"Not that I know of," Pacie said. "And by the way, Slenderman is not a person, it's a thing."

Detective Wanat just looked at Pacie. "Do you mind going down to the police station so that we can make a formal statement?"

"Sure, I can do that." Then Pacie said, "This all happened back at that mansion in the woods. I think you're familiar with it?"

Detective Wanat nodded but added nothing more.

"There's some dimensional thing or time travel stuff going on back there. Anna and the others are still in one of those dimensions. The one where the mansion is like brand new."

Detective Wanat gave a knowing look, as though she knew about the place but did not want to elaborate. "I would suggest you and Irma keep it to yourselves and not go back there again."

"How long have you known about it?"

"A while. Few people know and we want to keep it that way."

"We?"

"We. And let's leave it at that."

"Pacie," Johnny shouted as he ran up to her with a paramedic at his side. "Thank god you're alright."

"I'm fine. Just a little, I mean a lot shook up, but I'll make it," Pacie said as a paramedic began cleansing and dressing her arm.

"You'll need stitches," the paramedic said as he taped the gauze into place. "

"What about Mr. Dibble?" Pacie said, pointing toward the dog's bleeding head.

Mr. Dibble held still while the paramedic treated the gash on his head. "He'll be okay."

Detective Wanat began walking toward the trail where other officers were gathering. "After you get your stitches, don't forget to head to the police station for a report. I won't be there; I have some arrests to make."

"You're going to the mansion?" Pacie asked, holding her painful arm next to her body.

With a nod and a lopsided smile, Det. Wanat turned away and joined the officers on the trail.

Irma ran up and joined them. She gasped when she saw blood on Pacie's clothes and the dressing on the top of Mr.

Dibble's head. "You and Mr. Dibble got hurt? Is Slenderman gone? Did you find the teenagers? Are the cops going to the mansion? I want you to tell me all about it."

With Pacie and Mr. Dibble bandaged up, they walked joyfully to the parking lot.

"You know, Pacie," Johnny said, holding her waist. "You should've told me what you and Irma were planning to do. You could've been injured even worse than you are. Or god forbid, have been killed."

"Yes, you're right," Pacie said. "But if I had told you, you wouldn't have let me go. And if I couldn't go, then the kids would not have been saved."

Johnny shook his head. "I guess you have a point."

"That's why I don't tell you quite *everything*," Pacie said with a wink.

Johnny shook his head. "Don't tell me. I don't want to know."

"Hey, guys," Irma said, looking upward. "Have you noticed that the fog is going away? I think the worst is over."

Pacie gave Irma a playful nudge. "Don't go jinxing us."

Irma reached into her pouch and took out a cigarette and lighter. "I guess it's safe to smoke now."

Pacie laughed. "I'll let Father Murphy know he helped us defeat Slenderman, and you to quit smoking, at least for a little while."

The storm had passed, leaving a rosy peach sunset that melted into a dark, malignant sky. The air smelled of fresh earth. An American robin sang cheery-up, cheery-oh while a buzzard soared overhead. The Emerald City evergreens that bordered the parking lot oozed remnants of the wicked, muddled fog.

THE END OF SLENDERMAN

CONNIE MYRES

MY NAME IS MR. DIBBLE

A Companion Short Story To The Novel Slenderman

My Name Is Mr. Dibble is a companion short story to the novel Slenderman: Pacie Rose Mysteries. It is told from one of the main characters' beloved pet dog's point of view. Mr. Dibble's master is Irma, the novel's quirky sidekick. He tells about a time when Slenderman paid a visit to his owner and what he did about it.

Mr. Dibble is based on a Staffordshire terrier, a member of my family. His name is Ham, beloved pet.

Enjoy!

CONNIE MYRES

Chapter 1

MY NAME IS MR. Dibble.

Some people, like my owner's cousin, call me a Staffie. Some call me an AmStaff. While others cower in fear, telling Master Irma to keep her pit bull away from them. They see my muscles and think I'm going to tear them to shreds. This makes me laugh. I bet you didn't know that dogs can laugh. I'm laughing now.

But I'm a Staffordshire terrier. A good-natured and smart canine with more courage than any other dog I know. I'm a loyal and trustworthy friend to Master Irma. She says I can be a little stubborn, but that's mostly when I'm hunting a squirrel, groundhog, or a pesky cat.

Miss Alley Cat, that's what I call her, is a wild one. She teases me, trying to get me to chase her. I do, of course. It's one of my jobs. When she scratches her way up a tree, little ol' Miss Alley Cat taunts me and laughs. Yes, cats can laugh, too. At least it looks like it to me.

I spend most of my time at Master Irma's side. She lets me rest on the couch while she works, but sometimes she makes me get up so she can put down my blanket. A doggy blanket, she calls it. Master thinks my feet are dirty or I'm going to leave a hair on a cushion. I think she gets a little carried away.

Master takes me for walks and sometimes for car rides. I love riding in the car almost as much as chasing Miss Alley Cat. I'm laughing again.

If I'm lucky, Master will take me on a case with her. Most of the time I'm stuck in the car. But there have been times when I have helped solve the case. I'll tell you about me and my good nose and ears later.

Anyway, that is a little bit about me.

My name is Mr. Dibble, the pampered.

Chapter 2

WHAT? MASTER IRMA IS talking in her sleep again? It certainly makes my ears perk up, lying here at her side. This is not normal for her. Sure, occasionally she mumbles, rolls over, then snores again. She says sometimes when I'm sleeping my legs move like I'm chasing a rabbit. I believe her, I probably am dreaming of chasing a rabbit, or Miss Alley Cat.

This is different. Her legs are moving like she's running. I'm sure something is chasing her because she does not take me for a jog—she can't run and smoke a cigarette at the same time. I worry she'll have a heart attack. Then what would happen to me? I would go for help, of course, and then be at her hospital bedside. But after that, I don't know.

I can see good in the dark. Lately, there's been a tall dark shadow that appears in the bedroom's corner, but only for a short while, and only while she's doing what she's doing now. I don't see it at the moment.

What is she doing? Master is sitting on the edge of the bed. She's saying she can't kill something. This is not my master speaking.

She's standing up, I'm going to follow her.

Wait, what? Master is leaving the apartment, and she's not taking her keys. And she's barefoot. Where is she going in the middle of the night?

She didn't even put my leash on me. I like that part.

Master is going outside, and she's not closing the doors behind her. I bet Miss Alley Cat would love to sneak up to my home and surprise me. But if she did that, I would easily catch her. I don't know what I'd do with her when I caught her. I would chalk one up for me and let her go. Master would kick her out of the house. I'd be laughing again.

Where is Master going? I can't believe she just stepped on that piece of glass and didn't flinch. Something is wrong.

We're going down the sidewalk to the lake. I like water, but I don't think she should swim right now.

Good, we're going to walk on the pier toward the lighthouse.

I don't think she's paying attention to where she's going. And I think her eyes are closed. But I could be wrong. Normally she takes breaks, but not now.

There is mist in the air and something that smells of rotten fish. Of course, it could be rotten fish, but my nose tells me it's something different.

The lighthouse isn't far away, but there is something dark standing next to it, like a tall human. This is bad news. Most humans who are out late at night are up to no good. I have to warn Master Irma.

I'm barking, but she's not listening. I'll run to that—thing. I don't think it's a human. I'm sure it is going to make Master do something terrible.

Stopping in front of Master to block her path is futile, she keeps walking into me. I have to move or I'll knock her over the edge of the pier and into the black water.

I have to attack it. I'll bite into it like it's a troublesome groundhog. I've gotten those before when we lived on the farm. Praise would stream my way for stopping the rodent from burrowing into the barn's foundation and for eating vegetables in the garden.

Now before me is the most terrifying enemy. Not necessarily to me, but to my master. It has wicked deeds planned for her. I will rip its heart out if I have to. And I can do it.

I'm baring my teeth and growling. I'm ready to attack.

My name is Mr. Dibble, the intimidator.

Chapter 3

MASTER IRMA HAS FINALLY stopped, but I can tell this thing is controlling her. I think I can hear what this faceless evil is telling her. It is just like what she was saying in her sleep, that she can not kill. I think it will kill her, though, if she does not do what it says.

I'm springing for its neck. I have it. I'm clenched into its neck muscles and jugular vein, twisting and biting. I can tell you I am glad it is not a shadow or I would fly off the pier and fall many feet into the churning water below.

The smell of coppery blood is not present, but I can for sure tell you where the rotten fish smell was originating from.

It's trying to pull me off by opening my jaws, but no one has stronger chops than I.

Now it's squeezing me, trying to crush my bones and pull out my innards. But my muscles are hard. No one is brawnier than I.

My name is Mr. Dibble, the beast.

Chapter 4

DANG! THE THING JUST vanished. Good thing I'm good on my feed.

I hear whimpering. Turning around, I see Master sitting on the concrete. She must be waking up. I'll lick her face and tell her how happy I am that she is alright.

As expected, she pushed me away. I don't know why she doesn't like wet kisses. There are not many ways that I can show her how much I love her.

Master is standing, and she is not very steady on her feet. I barked once to let her know that I am paying attention.

She's confused and wondering why we are here, standing next to the lighthouse in the dark and gloom. I want to tell her I just saved her life, but I think she already knows.

Master Irma hugged me and then I proudly led her back down the pier, through a developing icy drizzle. The monster is gone, at least for now. I know it will return. When it does, I'll recruit Miss Alley Cat to lay some claws on it while I finish the job I started. We will both be laughing.

My name is Mr. Dibble, the protector.

CONNIE MYRES

THE END OF MY NAME IS MR. DIBBLE

JEZEBEL

A Companion Short Story To The Novel Slenderman

An antique shop owner buys a nineteenth-century doll with a deadly history.

When an eccentric man brings in an old doll that he wants off his hands, Johnny, the antique shop owner, takes him up on the deal. The doll is beautiful with red lips and auburn hair. Johnny becomes affectionate toward it, giving it the name, Jezebel. When Johnny's girlfriend, Pacie, shows up, unexpected events begin to happen.

CONNIE MYRES

Chapter 1

JOHNNY FINISHED POLISHING HIS latest acquisition, an English silver teapot. He looked up from his workbench at the back of the shop, behind the cash register, when the entrance doorbell jingled. He was not surprised, much, when a man with the tips of his hair dyed blue and a ring on every finger walked inside the shop with a gate like that of a slinky cat. He held something wrapped in newspaper in his hands as he walked up to the counter.

"May I help you?" Johnny said, washing his hands.

"I have something I want to sell." He sat the package on the countertop.

Johnny walked up to the counter. "What do you have?"

The man began unwrapping the newspaper with his fingertips as if it were contaminated. Inside was an antique doll.

"That's a lovely bisque doll. How long have you had it?"

"Too long," the man said. "I'll give you a deal on it."

Johnny picked up his jeweler's magnifier that sat next to the old-fashioned cash register. "May I examine it?"

"Be my guest." The man stepped back.

Johnny bent over the doll and mumbled, "French bisque head. 1889. Looks like human hair. Red. French hat and dress. Leather boots. About two feet high. Excellent condition." He looked up. "What are you asking for it?"

"I'm not sure."

"What did you pay for it?"

"Three thousand dollars at an auction."

"Why are you selling it?"

The man crossed his arms. "I don't want it anymore."

"I'm sorry for asking these questions." Johnny could tell the man was uncomfortable. "I'm just trying to figure its worth."

The man said nothing for a moment. He shook his head and backed up some more. "It's not for me. It's not my style. I just don't like it."

Johnny looked the doll over a bit more, then said, "If you give me a price, I'd be happy to take it off your hands."

"A hundred bucks," the man said. "I just want it out of my house before I throw it in the trash."

Surprised by the man's hateful reaction to the exquisite doll, he said, "I'll give you a thousand dollars, which is significantly less than it is worth. I don't want to steal it from you."

The man nodded.

Johnny prepared the paperwork for the man and paid him. Johnny was now the owner of a doll that had more to its history than the man was saying.

Chapter 2

"THERE YOU GO, MY beautiful," Johnny said, placing the collectible doll on a shelf inside the lighted glass case next to the service counter. It pleased him to see its red lips from his work area. He turned when he heard someone come in the back door. It was Pacie. "Look what I just added to the shop."

Pacie looked at the doll in the case. "I like it. Where did you get it?"

Johnny kissed her, then said, "A quite unusual guy sold it to me today. He didn't want it anymore. He acted like he was afraid of it?"

"Really? Why?"

Johnny turned back to the doll and smiled. "I don't know why. But I do find it quite attractive."

Pacie leaned into him. "Don't get carried away, Romeo, it's only a doll."

"I love *you*, Pacie. Don't you forget it." Johnny pulled her close to his body.

"I know you do." She kissed him, then looked at the doll.

Johnny saw her gaze frozen on the doll's porcelain face.

"What's wrong."

Pacie shrugged. "Nothing. I just thought it frowned at me, but I know that's impossible."

Johnny laughed. "Frowned at you? You do realize it's not real."

"Of course."

"Or are you jealous of Jezebel's kissable lips, adoring eyes, and creamy skin?"

"No, but I think you're in love with it. Do *you* realize it's not real? And why did you give it a name?"

Johnny put his hands in his pockets. "You're funny, Pacie. Hey, do you mind watching the store while I bring in a few things from the truck? I have a box of assorted trinkets that I got at an estate sale."

"Sure."

Pacie watched Johnny walk out the back door as she moseyed around the shop, looking and touching items as she walked past them. When she reached the front window, she looked out onto the rather dreary main street of Black Water. The weather was dismal. Few people strode the sidewalks.

A tap at the back of the shop caught Pacie's attention. She turned around, hoping it was Johnny, but he was not back inside, yet. She moved toward the counter where she thought the sound came from and noticed the cute little doll dressed in an apron and bonnet, next to Johnny's red-lipped beauty, had somehow fallen forward and now rested against the glass door.

Pacie carefully opened the door, catching the little doll before it fell to the floor. With care, she placed it back in its spot. Before closing the case door she looked at Jezebel and touched its auburn hair. It was a lovely doll but there was something odd about it, but she could not figure out what was causing her uneasy feeling toward it.

Johnny walked back inside the shop and placed a box on top of the counter.

"This doll's hair feels so real," Pacie said, rolling it between her fingers.

Johnny walked up next to her. "That's because it is."

"What? This is real human hair?" Pacie at once closed the case door.

Johnny laughed. "Got a problem with it?"

"Yeah, I think I do." Pacie stepped away from the display case. "Not from a dead person, I hope."

"Well, they're dead now. This is a really old doll."

Pacie shivered. "So you're telling me I was just touching a dead woman's hair. There's something plain wrong with that."

"It's an antique doll. What did you expect?"

"Not that." Pacie turned to the box that Johnny had brought in. "What's in there?"

Johnny folded open the flaps of the cardboard box. "I'm not sure. Just a bunch of junk, probably. I got it real cheap at the auction. Sometimes there's something valuable mixed in with the worthless items. I have another box to bring in. I'll be right back."

Pacie looked inside the half-filled box and began rummaging through its content. Tarnished cutlery, small plates, and assorted items that would fit in a kitchen's junk drawer were all it contained. "Johnny's right, it's a bunch of junk."

Toward the bottom of the box, Pacie pulled out an old

cookbook; more like a pamphlet of recipes requiring baking powder. She began flipping through the pages. A sudden bang on the glass door of the display case made Pacie jump. She turned. Jezebel's arms were raised, and its head turned as if it was staring at Pacie.

Johnny came back into the shop and sat the box he was carrying on the back workbench. He looked at Pacie, who was pointing at the case. "What's wrong. You look like you've seen a ghost."

"There's something wrong with that doll. Do you remember seeing that doll with its arms raised like that?"

Johnny walked up to the case and removed the doll. "No, but it could be the weather. Possibly the humidity is tightening or stretching things, causing them to move."

"Are you sure there are no mechanical parts inside of it?"

Johnny flipped it over and looked at the neck and back underneath the doll's clothes. "There's nothing here."

"That doll gives me the creeps."

Johnny stroked its hair and kissed its cheek. "You're imagining things, Pacie."

Pacie sighed. "I think that doll has control over you. Like you're in love with it. Or she's in love with you."

"Have you been drinking?" Johnny sat the doll on the counter next to the box Pacie had been looking through. He looked at the booklet in Pacie's hand. "Did you get that from the box?"

"Yeah, it's an old cookbook." She handed it to Johnny.

Johnny studied the recipe book for a moment. "It's not worth much. You can keep it if you want."

"Thanks." Pacie looked at the doll, lying motionless on the countertop. She turned her back to it and leaned against the counter.

Johnny ran the back of his hand along her cheek. "I'm head over heels in love with you, Pacie."

"You'd better tell that to Jezebel." Pacie kissed him.

"I gotta get back to work," Johnny said. "We'll finish this later."

"Promise?"

"Promise," Johnny whispered in her ear. He walked back to his work desk.

Pacie leaned back against the counter and thumbed through the old cookbook. The clink of metallic objects inside the box on the counter behind her made her turn around. "I think you brought a mouse into the shop."

"I'm not surprised," Johnny said, busy working.

"Hey, Johnny."

"What?"

"Did you move the doll?"

"Wow, you're obsessed with Jezebel. I sat her on the counter. Remember?"

Pacie swallowed hard. "I hate to tell you this, but she's not there."

Chapter 3

"SHE'S RIGHT THERE ON the counter, on the other side of the box," Johnny said, turning around. He took off his magnifying glasses. "Very funny, what did you do with her?"

"Nothing. She's not there nor in the display case." Pacie moved away from the counter.

Johnny stood up.

A sharp pain in Pacie's thigh made her scream. She looked down and saw Jezebel holding a knife. The doll's eyes glowed red as it thrust the bloody knife back and forth into Pacie's thigh, causing her to fall to the floor. She frantically crawled away from the doll who was pursuing her with the knife raised, ready to jab.

Johnny rushed up and grabbed the doll. He stuffed it in the box and immediately sealed it with tape. The doll stabbed at the box from the inside.

"It's going to escape," Pacie said, trying to stop the bleeding with her hand.

Johnny grabbed a vintage wool scarf from a shelf and wrapped it around Pacie's leg. "Are you gonna be alright?

I have to figure out what to do with Jezebel before she escapes."

"Do what you have to do, I'll be fine," Pacie said, keeping pressure on the wounds.

Johnny stared at the box for a moment, trying to decide what to do with the doll before it broke free. He could see the tip of the knife ripping through the brown cardboard. But what to do?

"Burn it," Pacie said.

Johnny grabbed the box. The tip of the knife was stabbing his hands as he ran out of the store with it. He tossed it in the dumpster and took the lighter from his pocket. Thank god for Irma needing a light every now and then. He set fire to newspapers and anything he could set ablaze inside the dumpster as the doll emerged from the box.

Jezebel climbed up the inside of the dumpster, its pale skin blackening as the fire spread over it.

Pacie limped up to Johnny and clung to him. "Do something."

"Sorry, Jezebel," Johnny said before punching the melting face, thrusting it back into the fire.

Pacie did not want to take her eyes off the doll. She wanted to see it burn, see it die, and not escape.

Distant sirens sounded.

Pacie looked away from the doll when Johnny picked her up and sat her on the tailgate of his pickup. "The firetruck will be here soon. Keep your leg elevated"

When the firefighters arrived and extinguished the fire, a paramedic tended to Pacie's leg. "What happened, ma'am?"

Pacie did not want to say that a doll stabbed her. Who

would believe such a thing? "It's a long story."

"Did someone do this to you?" The paramedic asked, glancing at Johnny who was talking with a firefighter.

"No, no one did this to me. I, I accidentally ran into something sharp in the shop."

"Sounds like it's dangerous in there."

"Not where the customers go. In the back of his workshop. I was being clumsy."

The paramedic looked at her. "If I didn't know better, I'd say you're pulling my leg. But if that's your story, that's what I'll record."

Pacie smiled. "That's my story."

"Okay, you're all bandaged up. You should see the doctor; you'll need some stitches. Do you want to go by ambulance?"

Pacie wanted to see the doll and make sure it was dead. "Johnny will take me."

"As you wish, ma'am."

When everyone left, Johnny took a shovel from the shop and began moving aside smoldering debris.

"Is it in there?" Pacie asked.

"I don't know. I don't see it."

"Do you think it ran away?"

Johnny stopped moving the garbage aside and looked intently at Pacie. "After what just happened, I do."

"I hope it's dead?" Pacie said, looking inside the dumpster.

"I still can't find it."

"Could it have been burned to ashes?"

"I hope so, but I don't see any hair, clothing, or remnants of any sort of the doll."

Pacie looked around the outside of the dumpster. Then she noticed the shop's back door was ajar. "Johnny, you don't think—"

They rushed inside the building and stopped when they heard climbing on the steps to the apartments. They ran to the staircase and saw the charred doll climbing the steps.

Johnny ran up to it. Jezebel turned its partially melted face toward him; its eyes and lips still red. "Better luck next time, babe." Johnny thrust the shovel blade through its neck, severing the head from the body.

Irma opened her apartment door and she and Mr. Dibble walked out. "What on earth are you two doing? I was watching the fire department through the window. Is that a burned doll?"

Johnny picked up the doll parts and took them outside. He jabbed the doll until it was now in several pieces. He tossed the parts into the dumpster. He ran into the shop and brought out a can of turpentine. He squirted the flammable liquid over the doll and then lit it on fire. Unnatural flames flared several feet above the dumpster until finally dying out.

Irma walked up to the dumpster and peered inside. "I believe you just killed a haunted doll. Maybe I'm not so fond of living above an antique shop."

Pacie and Johnny laughed until Mr. Dibble walked around the dumpster with a doll leg in his mouth.

"Can't be," Pacie said.

Johnny took the leg from Mr. Dibble. "I don't think so. Looks like it belongs to another doll."

"Did you throw out other doll pieces?" Pacie asked.

"No. But someone else could've. I'm not the only one who

uses the dumpster," Johnny said.

"You need a new profession." Pacie winced as she grabbed her aching leg. "And you need to take me to get stitches."

"I'll get my keys and we'll head out," Johnny said, walking to the shop.

Irma walked up to Pacie. "Tell Johnny not to buy any more dolls."

"You got it," Pacie said as she leaned on Irma and limped to the passenger side of Johnny's pickup. "I think I'm even going to throw out my childhood teddy bear."

The End of Jezebel

Thank you for reading!

https://www.ConnieMyres.com

Read the Next Book in the Series

HORNET: PACIE ROSE MYSTERIES, #2

A citizen reporter must stop hummingbird-sized hornets from destroying a resort town before the government unleashes its own devious scheme to eliminate them.

When a swarm of murder hornets invades a Lake Michigan resort town, citizen reporter Pacie Rose and her sidekick cousin struggle to find what is causing mutant stinging wasps, now grown to the size of hummingbirds, from attacking the residents of Black Water, while also working against an aggressive, and unwelcome, secret government plot that could do as much if not more harm to the residents as the killer hornets in this natural horror.

Get the book at <u>ConnieMyres.com</u> or your favorite online store.

Also by Connie Myres

STAND-ALONE BOOKS & STORIES

Jezebel • My Name is Mr. Dibble • Ring • Haunting of Ender House • Rest Stop Terror • Solus • Who Killed Sweet Violet? • Lucifer's Island • Raven's Ridge

PACIE ROSE MYSTERIES

Slenderman • Hornet

RANCOR

Rancor: A Paranormal Psychological Thriller (Books 1 & 2) Sinister Attachments • Unrestrained

SEVEN SEALS REDUX

Seven Seals Redux: The Complete Apocalyptic Novel Series (Books 1-7) White Horse • Red Horse • Black Horse • Pale Horse • Tribulation • Signs • Trumpets

SUSPENSE STORIES

Suspense Stories #1: Raven's Ridge, Lucifer's Island, Sinister Attachments (Suspense Stories, #1)

THREE SISTERS ODYSSEY (SERIAL)

Read Episodes As Connie Writes Them on Kindle Vella

WATCH FOR SPOOKY SHORTS

A collection of creepy short stories, A-Z.

Spooky Shorts A-G: A Collection of Creepy Short Stories
Apple Pie • Black-Eyed Kids • Creature • Dungeon • Electric
• Fairy • Genie • House • Ice • Joker • Kiss • Lucid • Minion
• Neighbor • Obelisk • Pattern • Quest • Rumor • Squatch •
Time • Underworld • Visitor • Wolf • X-axis • Yellow • ZoZo.

Find an updated book list at <u>ConnieMyres.com</u> or your
favorite online bookstore.

About the Author

CONNIE MYRES writes books and short stories in the horror, mystery, suspense, and science fiction genres. She is an author, developer, and registered nurse. Sometime in the future—whether by choice or by arm-twisting—she will join the digital nomad movement.

Born and raised in Michigan, she has been creating stories since childhood. Children she had babysat as a teenager loved to hear her mystery stories, especially since she carefully included all the children listening into the storyline, causing suspense for everyone.

Connie's website: https://www.ConnieMyres.com

Feather and Fermion Publishing

Founded in 2014, Feather and Fermion Publishing proudly publishes horror, mystery, suspense, thriller, science fiction and fantasy stories. Our imprints—Oort Cloud Books and White-Knuckle Books—publish original fiction with the mission to entertain readers.

Author Connie Myres owns Feather and Fermion Publishing.

Visit Connie's Website

Visit Connie's website and find her blog, books, ARC team, movies, podcast, and where you can follow her on social media.

ConnieMyres.com

www.ingramcontent.com/pod-product-compliance
Lightning Source LLC
Chambersburg PA
CBHW031156050726
47495CB00019B/1886